A Week on the
Beach

A Week on the
Beach

by

Cab Doyle

authorHOUSE®

AuthorHouse™
1663 Liberty Drive
Bloomington, IN 47403
www.authorhouse.com
Phone: 1-800-839-8640

This story is fictional and does not depict any actual persons or events

First published by AuthorHouse   09/16/2011

ISBN: 978-1-4634-4390-0 (sc)
ISBN: 978-1-4670-4167-6 (ebk)

Printed in the United States of America

Any people depicted in stock imagery provided by Thinkstock are models, and such images are being used for illustrative purposes only.
Certain stock imagery © Thinkstock.

This book is printed on acid-free paper.

Dedicated to Summer

Arrival of the Barbarians

Sunday is turnover day for my beach rentals. And as I do every Sunday, I keep an eye on the Brazilian housekeepers as they pretend to clean. No elbow grease in those arms. They just laze around with their cigarettes and illegitimate mulloto children, forever blabbing in their foreign tongues into cell phones. But they stop when they see me. I may be an old woman, but they put the phones away when they see me coming. I stay right on top of 'em, making sure they scrub the toilets. Otherwise, they wouldn't.

'Course, you see incoming tenants waiting yonder in their gas guzzlers with the engines running, on their cell phones, kids watching TV in the car, *television in the car,* like they can't do without TV *for a few hours????* Junk food scattered all over the floor. Pigs!

No manners! Loud! Brazen! On motorcycles! Half-breeds with tattoos come to my beach and act like a bunch of *heathens!*

What a bunch of fat, lazy slobs calling themselves Americans. Sitting on giant rear ends on my beach!

They trot sand directly into my houses! They don't even bother to rinse off!

Sand is the enemy of my rental houses. But sand fills every crevice, thanks to the slop-headed tenants who pass by my outdoor showers. They walk right in, covered with sand, don't even LOOK at the outdoor showers! They walk right into the house! *I watch them!* I see them do it! Their kids bring in *buckets of sand* and dead starfish! Right into the living room! They shake sand off their bodies like wet dogs! They trot right in, their ankles *caked* with sand, their *mothers never taught them to wipe their feet????* It is a *disgrace!*

And when the tenants leave, my Brazilian housekeepers, or as I like to call them, *The Illegals, steal* whatever the tenants leave behind. And the tenants are so lazy, so *wasteful,* they leave all their food behind. So The Illegals clean out the refrigerators, taking the eggs, butter, ketchup, jars of mayonnaise, jelly and relish. They take the cans and the mixes and porterhouse steaks and cases of beer and half-drunk bottles of booze. They steal away with the left-behind tennis racquets, beach chairs, roller skates, binoculars, prescriptions, *anything!* One brown skin with a gold front tooth grabbed a canoe! A Coleman canoe! Beautiful! Brand new! This stupid family from Chicago left it behind. They said they couldn't fit it in their car, the idiots! They didn't even try. I saw them. And the Illegals grabbed it! 'Course they did! They'd take the fillings from your teeth, if you fell asleep with your mouth open.

This new crop of tenants are a bunch of beach amateurs. They ride in like the Beverly Hillbillies, those ridiculous gas-sucking trucks piled high with plastic boats and contraptions, strollers, barbeques, bicycles and surfboards! Stupid to bring all that stuff. They never use it. They get to my beach and there they sit. On those big fat fannies of theirs.

Tenderfoots hop across the sand, like that one right over there, look at that woman's fanny! Dear God! She must need a forklift to sit on a toilet. Look at her fat children! And look, she's opening up a bag and handing out sandwiches! Dear God! *What is this country coming to?*

They set up their encampments too close to others, they swim out too far, they shake their sandy towels in the wind. They trod over sand castles and *feed the goddamn seagulls!* No sense! No manners!

Barbarians!

But for three thousand bucks a week, I'll put up with 'em.

1 *Memories*

Beach Rock cottage is just as I remembered it. Unfortunately, nothing much has changed in those 25 years. I'm sorriest for myself to say, the cottage is in its original state. No improvements have been made. And I'm sorry because I am about to get yelled at for renting these houses, even though I did all the work, finding the realtor, the houses, mailing and what have you.

The rental agent had been iffy about air conditioning, and I suppose I'm lucky to have even gotten these cottages. But still, you pay that amount of money and find yourself renting a house with a greasy, yellowed electric stove . . . well, it's a let down, you know? And a front porch with yard sale furniture—well, I'm gonna catch a rain of shit, that's all.

"It's about the view," the realtor had said. And she's right. The view of the beach is spectacular. Epic. I look at the water and I'm flooded with happiness. I even think to myself, it won't hurt us to "rough it" for a week.

This summer, Richard has indulged me with a vacation of my choice—instead of the Jersey Shore. He and the kids whine, of course—all of their friends are at The Shore. But when do I get something *I want?* Right. Never. So Miner's Beach, here we are! See, I am so sick of trying to please everybody else, dammit, it's time I pleased myself. And that's what this vacation is all about. I'm off duty, I'm turning off the cell phone and doing what I want.

I carry-in bags of groceries, cartons of my favorite pans and my Cuisinart, of course. Gotta bring the Cuisinart! Richard and the kids pass me guilty over-the-shoulder glances as they race into the ocean.

No air conditioning. So I stand in front of a plastic fan and drip. And console myself with a chocolate cupcake. Chocolate is the love of my life! With a glass of cold milk. But when I open the cabinet, the glass is one of those cloudy old cartoon jelly jars. A yard sale acquisition. I pull open a drawer, mottled gray utensils and mis-matched silverware roll toward me. What is this? The whole house is equipped with yard sales left-behinds!

I can't find a single lobster claw cracker or seafood pick. Luckily I brought my own. A cabinet yields thin Correll plates, the orange flower collection.

I hear the honking of a horn. Glancing out the cottage window, I see my sister-in-law's white Escalade crunching over our shared clamshell driveway. I run out to the porch.

"Marcie! Over here!" I wave. She doesn't respond. She squints. She's looking at me but not seeing me, I guess.

"Marce!" I grin and wave as she parks.

Her twin girls and son erupt from the SUV and race to the beach. She gingerly steps out, "This is the place?" she questions aloud. The line of her mouth indicates disenchantment. Uh-oh. I hurry down the back steps. Behind her Chanel sunglasses, she's hard to read, but when I'm standing right in front of her, she shakes her head with surprise and happily shares a hug. "Aw, Candy! It's so good to see you!"

"So glad you made it. Hope you didn't get lost!"

This arrangement has been so for years. Marcie and Jack, Richard and I, our combined five kids, renting side-by-side beach houses. Only this year we were trying a new shoreline in Wintusket, Massachusetts.

I dearly love my sister in law. Marcie and I have shared so many things, our dream-come-true weddings, the thrill of building our new homes, growing families—I always call her for advice or just to vent, or laugh at our latest motherly debacles. She has decorating ideas and funny stories about the women in her tennis club.

More than anything, I adore her because Marcie is my husband's little sister. She's my sister-in-law sorority sister and good buddy. We call each other and gab while watching the Food Network. And I'll admit, we're both helicopter Moms, but today, you kind of have to be, you know?

We keep schedules and lists and navigate our families from pediatricians' offices to soccer tournaments, dancing lessons to parent teacher conferences. Both of us are key players in the parent teacher organizations, Cupcakes for Class, Teacher Appreciation Week, and cookies for bake sales. My frequently requested "Candy Store" cookies—the size of Frisbees—are now legendary in our town! My own secret recipe: sugar cookie dough embedded with pieces of candy bars, macadamia, mini-marshmallows, cashew nuts, chips of butterscotch, caramel, peanut butter, Rice Krispies, pretzel sticks, raisins and Milk Duds. Only Marcie knows this secret recipe! Now that's sisterly love.

"Lookie what you brought! Pinot Grigio!" I hoot as I hoist a large bottle of Marcie's favorite wine into the beach house next door. "Mommy's time-out!"

Her sunglasses removed, her eyes pierce me. "Ohhhhhh boy! This mommy can really use a time-out! The kids were crazy in the car! They only brought one DVD and it kept skipping!"

Marcie winks at me, pulling two Betsy McCall matching duffle bags on wheels, her biceps buff, her dark blonde hair pulled back in a cool pony tail, her trim figure in a pink and green Lilly Pulitzer shift. She's lean and tan and anxious as she surveys the house, biting her lip. "This place is . . . a little . . . rustic."

"Yep, it's no frills." I act like it isn't a big deal. See, because I know what's coming.

"It's very . . . back to basics," she murmurs, her brows furl as she swipes at a spider web in the doorjamb. Marcie's getting really wrinkly from all that tennis and tanning and exercise. She should watch it. At the same time, she could pass for one of the Housewives of Beverly Hills, she looks so well-tended.

"One thing's for sure. The kids won't starve this week." Changing the subject, combing my frizzy bangs from my eyes, I hold the door open for her. "Maybe your place has an air conditioner."

Marcie rolls her wide blue eyes. "It sure ain't looking that way. This carpet is older than I am," Marcie gripes. She surveys the dated wallpaper darkly. Her shoulders droop as we enter the kitchen. A harvest gold electric stove from the 1970's, a refrigerator meant for a college dorm room. Right away, she reacts, *"Oh no no no no no . . . ."*

"Aw well, it's not a cook's kitchen, but—"

Her mouth is hanging open, she's shaking her head, "I'm not paying three thousand bucks for this." Marcie's all-powerful "How-Could-You-Let-Me-Down" Look.

"Before you make up your mind Marcie, take a look over here. Come on. *Over here! This* is why we're here! The beach." I motion her out onto the front porch. As she passes through the threshold, she brightens at the immensity of the beach at the foot of the steps. A wave crashes and a sweep of foam unfolds over the sand. A sole runner and his dog gallop along the ocean's edge. A beach free of fried dough peddlers, tattoo parlors and carny people.

"Oh! Wow! This is nice. Look at that big rock!"

"That's Miner's Rock. That one to the left is called Diver's. And over to the right, that's called Elephant."

"Elephant?"

"If you look to the side, it's shaped just like an elephant's head."

"I'll take your word for it." Marcie folds her arms, her mouth slackens, weighing her options. I quickly change the subject.

"Where's Jack?" For a split second, I notice a shadow pass over Marcie's face as she quickly answers, "He's driving up after work."

"He's working on a *weekend?*"

"He's ironing out a deal on a book adaptation." Marcie re-adjusts her tight ponytail. I notice her blonde highlights are as perfectly measured as a picket fence.

"But still." I cock my head to the side. "I just don't like the strange hours Jack keeps."

Me and my big mouth. Marcie sighs, "Please."

Looking away from me, she kneels and zips open a bag, yanks out a bright red swimsuit. Walks to the bathroom, hollering over her shoulder. "Candy, we'll talk later about this rental. Right now, I have to get in that water or I'll faint. I am dying here. This place is like a furnace."

Oh great. Now she's mad at me.

"But you're okay with this place?" I pry from behind the bathroom door.

"Coming from Camden, being raised there, I'm equipped to deal with it. Okay with it? No. But it may be good for us until we find a new place. Okay Candy?"

She bursts open the door, fanning herself, I step back. She's crisp in her bright Land's End tankini.

"One thing at a time, and right now, it's cooling off!"

Then Marcie zithers past me, out of the bathroom, racing down the stairs and she runs, laughing past her children and dives cleanly into the ocean. The twins and Jack Junior speed after her, and they splash into her arms.

Maybe I should I join her? The cold water would feel so good. My immediate mind says no, of course not. I can barely fit into my swim suit. Plus, I need to tidy up. I should unpack for everyone, drive to the harbor and buy lobsters! But when I take another look at the ailing stove and the beaten gray aluminum lobster pot, I say to myself, "We'll eat out tonight."

I manage to squirm into my swimsuit, after practically getting trapped in it, trying to pull it over my head. Yes, okay, I know, I put on some weight after my foot surgery.

As I walk across the sand, I feel my thighs wapping against one another, my upper arms reverberate. I have to get back in touch with my Jenny Craig representative.

Shading my eyes, I see Richard's up ahead, body surfing.

"Hey, how's the water?" I smile. He doesn't see me.

I shout and wave to Richard. "Hey honey!"

Richard turns, squints toward me, then slowly turns away and dives into a towering oncoming wave. The sun was in his eyes, I guess.

2 The Cat's Away

A silver 911 GT 2 purrs along West 45th street, the City still dazed with heat and humidity. And even though the air conditioner blasts within the supple leather interior of the Porsche, the heat inside is palatable.

"I liked waking up next to you this morning," the twenty-something brunette whispers. "Oh God," her shoulders jerk back as the driver, carefully keeping his eyes on the road, slides his hand under her skirt. With a quick side glance, he notices her nipples harden under her tube top.

In turn, she slides her hand onto his lap.

"Whoa, hold on there Tonto. I'm driving."

He smiles and pulls over. He's an older guy, but he's not yet past his prime. Longish graying blonde hair. Handsome. Tanned. Hypnotic green eyes. "And here we are Miss, home sweet home."

Double-parked in front of her apartment building, she reaches for the strap of her leather over night bag. "I guess this is goodbye, for a week," she pouts.

He looks at her tiredly. "Gwen. We talked about this."

Her eyes fill. "This isn't fair you know."

He catches her tears before they splash on the leather seat. To distract her, he slips his hand into her panties. "Hey now—you're wrecking the great weekend we had. Didn't we have a great weekend?"

She sniffles. "Yup. I guess."

"Didn't you like staying at The Pierre?"

She brightens a little. "Yup. It was nice."

"The king size bed? The couples massage we had? The Jacuzzi?"

"That was hot." True.

Her good graces back in place, he leans forward and kisses her, his hand roaming.

"I love you," she whispers, a tone of reproach at the end of the word, 'you.' She waits for his answer. She doesn't get one. He's too busy enjoying the thrill of openly fingering her as traffic rolls by.

She removes his hand, readjusts her top and brusquely opens the car door. She pulls her skirt down, tersely reminding him, "Call me!"

"Don't call me!" he grins back, and she slams the door so hard, the car rocks.

3 *Making The Best of It*

Honestly, we could not get the kids off the beach. Candy and I had to drag them out of the water, begging them to get in the car. Their lips were purple. Even Richard gave us a hard time about leaving, but it was eight o'clock. Too hot to cook. Plus, we hadn't really unpacked all of our stuff and we just didn't want to. After all, it is vacation we reminded ourselves: this is Mommy's time out.

Richard, Candy, the kids and I had a late dinner at Hugo's Lighthouse. Jack called from the road in Providence. Guargantuan traffic jam on 95 north, he would be late, go ahead, he'd catch up with us. He didn't sound too thrilled about the house, of course *I'm not so thrilled* about the house either, and he hasn't even seen it yet. But according to Candy, we're locked into our leases and we may as well make the best of it.

I already called hotels while Candy was out of earshot and there are no vacancies locally. I don't want to bother with the crowds on The Cape or the Islands.

Jack liked the idea of climbing the rocks with the kids. I brought his kayak and fishing gear, so he sounded like he was looking forward to that.

The kids nibble a few bites of their chicken fingers and fries, spilling root beer all over the table, then tear off to play video games. "Don't run!"

"They raided my purse!" Candy whines. "I won't have any quarters for the laundromat."

I wilt at the prospect of doing laundry at a coin-op. "Oh, that's right! No washers or dryers. *And why did we rent these houses again?"*

Candy looks down at her lap, hurt, but I can't help it. I hate these houses. I pick at my oysters, ask the waitress for more sauce.

"Come on, Marcie! Make do, will ya? The kids love this beach."

"The beach is fine, the houses, frankly, suck . . ."

"Much less crowded than the Jersey Shore!" Candy cocks her head and raises her eyebrows.

"True but the houses suck! I feel like I'm trapped in hell."

Richard clasps his knee in folded hands and smiles with amusement. "It's only a week Marce. Seven days. You'll make it. It's not like you're staying in Haiti."

"This is like my own private Haiti."

Candy deflects my comments and puts her dinner napkin on the table. "Now if you two will excuse me. I'm off to the powder room."

When Candy waddles off, I whisper to Richard, "Dear God, what are you feeding that girl?"

Richard sighs and takes a long drink of his beer. "I know. She's never been this big. But, you know. She tries."

"Tries? Tries what? To kill herself?"

I can tell when my brother is lying and he's lying to me now. "Richard. Come on. You can't be okay with this?"

His forehead wrinkles. He's losing his hair, I notice. "I'm not saying that—I'm just saying . . . She did have that bunion surgery."

"Richard, she had that surgery because her feet are giving out under all that weight!"

Richard rubs his eyes. He sighs. "Marcie, I just can't. I can't . . ."

"Listen Richard. When we were skiing last winter, when Candy fell, she couldn't get up! We had to ski on without her."

"Look Marcie, just leave it alone."

"Richard. She fell and *she could not get up!*"

"I don't say anything about Jack—"

"We're not talking about me. And somebody's gotta say it!" A couple at a table to the left look at me. I'm talking too loud. I whisper and they turn back to their lobsters.

"She's obese!"

"You don't help her with your Food Network marathons," Richard whispers, embarrassed.

"She told me she joined Weight Watchers."

"I thought it was Jenny Craig," he stares at the neck of his beer bottle. "Any way, I'm thinking about—" And then I can't hear what Richard just said.

"What? I can't hear you."

Richard looks around leans forward, "Any way, I'm thinking about lee—Candy." I still can't hear him.

"Louder!" I cup my ear. "What was that?"

Richard's shoulders drop. "Never mind. Here she comes."

I sit back in my chair and pretend to look at the dessert menu. Richard drains his beer.

Observation: How to Spot A Beach Amateur

Beach amateurs feed seagulls.

They bring beach umbrellas.

They read broadsheet newspapers.

They play with Paddle ball sets.

Beach amateurs set up volleyball nets.

They shout into their cell phones, "Can you hear me now? What? I

said—I'm at the beach! I'm at the beach"

4 What the Eff?

Entering the front door, I'm hit by a wall of heat so intense, it stings the rims of my nostrils. I turn right around and flop into a porch chair, losing myself in the echoey desert of Miner's Beach. Not a soul around. The moonlight on the sand creates an otherworldly set. In the house, I can hear the kids whine as Candy sprays them with bug repellent, "Mom!!"

"Cover your eyes!"

"It stings!"

"I said cover your eyes!"

Every window is wide open, but the house is impervious to breeze.

The kids can't plug their video games into the 1970's TV sets, so they run to the ocean's edge.

Christ, these houses don't even have WIFI. But Candy's in heaven, placing a tray on the creaking wicker coffee table.

"Harvarti dill from Trader Joe's!" *How can she still be thinking about food?* She brings out a bowl of Doritos and red Twizzlers for the kids.

She pours my Pinot Grigio on ice, "Thank you!"

She cracks open a beer for Richard and pours a hefty glass of chardonnay for herself. Candy extends a cracker with a slice of cheese to me.

"Oh honestly Candy, I can't. I'm stuffed."

I'm secretly hoping tonight's oysters will ignite the old libido. Hoping Jack and I might have a little sex tonight. It's been so long.

Where is Jack?

I watch my brother sitting next to Candy, and he looks positively diminutive next to her. Candy pops the cracker in her mouth. I realize she reminds me of "Ord," a cartoon character on "Dragon Tales."

"This was where I had my first kiss, on this beach."

Amused, Richard lifts his eyebrows. "Really? *I thought I was your first.*"

"Who was your first kisser, Candy?" I lean back in my rocker. I put my arm on the one existing armrest.

She smiles, a glint in her eyes, she whips her long dark hair over one shoulder. Honestly, she has such a beautiful face, if I could just peel off those packets of flesh from her neck, her jaw line. Oh my God, Candy was so pretty in college, she was one of the most popular girls in our sorority. And now, well, I can barely recognize her. I mean, one of her thighs is the size of my waist.

"His name was John Brith. I told him I had learned how to kiss—and I wanted to teach him how." She chuckles.

"You hussy," I joke. I personally know that Candy's only slept with Richard.

"Right, I know. So I told him, just get really close to me and say, *prune.*" We all laugh.

"Prune? It really does make you purse your lips."

"Prune! Prooooooooooonne!"

"And he did. He leaned in, said *prune,* and I kissed him."

"You didn't go to second base?"

"Geez, Richard, I was five."

"Prude." I add, smiling.

"She is," Richard adds, not smiling.

"Now, now." Candy gazes out, the moonlight on the powdered sugar sand is riveting.

"Oh I loved being five, on this beach. I had a blue two-piece bathing suit, which I loved, naturally curly hair, and I distinctly remember thinking to myself, standing right over there on that rock, "I love being five!"

"Sure beats being thirty five." I croak.

Richard chimes in. "You're right. Five is a great age. School is really easy. You've mastered walking. You're not always banging your head on the kitchen table all the time. And you know nothing about taxes or colonoscopies."

"Ick, I don't want to think about colonoscopies." I pick up my iPhone and dial Jack. "*Honey? Hello?* Honest to God—I don't think—Look Candy! I'm not getting any reception! Maybe something's wrong with my phone?"

Candy languidly flings a hand toward the back of the house, toward the street, while swallowing her cheese. "I think you have to stand out in the road."

"What? I have to stand out in the *road? To make a fucking phone call?*" She flinches at my F-bomb.

"Candy? What the eff?"

Candy's annoyed. "Marcie! Just go down the steps, take a left and a left. Geez!" She turns away, munching some chips.

"Out in the road? To make a phone call? What the fuck is this!" I stand up.

Richard shakes his head, avoiding the unpleasantness. I exhale loudly, "I'll be back."

"That's what the Terminator said," Richard chuckles, trying to break the tension. Richard avoids confrontation like it's ebola.

Dialing Jack, rounding the house, I'm yelling into the phone and suddenly, up ahead, I spy Jack's car in the driveway. The engine is off, but he's sitting in there, talking on his cell phone. I walk up to the window. He's putting on the bracelet I gave him. I can barely hear him saying something like, "I'll call you when I can! No not tomorrow! *When I get a chance!*"

I knock on the window. Caught off guard, Jack's neck snaps around. He sees it's me, then his face expands into a smile. He shuts off his phone and opens the car door.

"Marce!" He gets out and kisses the top of my head. "Well, look at you in your preppie dress!" He shuts the car door and gives me a half hug. "You little prepster!"

"I was just trying to call you! Where have you been?" He walks to the rear and removes his bag.

"Oh come on Marce, give me a break. The traffic was a bitch and they're nagging me in LA. Christ, can't a guy go on vacation?"

"My poor guy." I put my arm around his waist. I love the fit of my shoulder against his rib cage. "Okay, prepare yourself. You are not going to like this house Jack."

"I promise I won't. Have we been drinking wine?"

"Guilty your honor."

"Look, I brought a great big bottle of whiskey."

"Good 'cause you're gonna need every drop." I note that his hair needs a trim. It looks lighter, for some reason.

We walk around the side of the house, arm in arm. I can barely match his long-legged steps. "Jack we should find out about moving to hotel. I bet it would cost the same."

"Oh it's just money. I'll make more." He kisses the top of my head.

"You bet you will. Listen, don't you think you should lock the car?"

"Marce will ya calm down? This ain't Amsterdam Avenue."

"Still, it's a Porsche."

"You're right." He turns, points and clicks his key remote toward the car 'til we hear the beep of the automatic locks.

"Done."

5 The Realization

The thing about it is, I'm not an alpha male. I'm not interested in building hierarchies or pissing contests or arm wrestling. I don't put on a show. Our house doesn't look like a palace. I drive a Volvo C70 coupe. It's nice. But it's not shouting out to the world what a cool happening guy I am. Because I'm not a cool, happening guy. I'm a grown-up. I am an executive in a mutual fund company. I'm a simple guy. And nothing goes further up my ass than a phony bastard. And unfortunately, that's just who my little sister Marcie married.

Jack walks up on the porch tonight, wearing a white silk shirt and a *bracelet* for God's sake, his usual good 'ole boy shit-eating grin, and I can tell he's fucking someone behind Marcie's back. *I can just tell.* And Marcie's standing there beaming at him, drinking her wine, completely clueless about what a pussy hound she's married.

"Richard." He shakes my hand, and through his slitty eyes, he knows that *I know* he's fooling around on my sister.

"Hey Jack. You made it. Traffic, eh?" I look that sly bastard right in the retinas. He doesn't answer.

"Welcome Jack!" Candy attempts to hug Jack but just puts his hand on her shoulder, mumbling something, then pulls away. "Oh Jack, it's so good to see you. Did you have dinner? Can I make you a sandwich?"

I can tell Jack is looking at Candy like, *oh my God she's as big as a Macy's Parade balloon!*

"Oh no thanks. I grabbed something on the road."

I refrain from saying, *"Oh, I'll bet you did."*

Instead, Marcie chimes in, "Jack, why don't I get you settled? We'll just pop over next door so I can unpack a little. Okay?"

Candy, ever the server, "Come back for dessert?"

"No thanks. We're tired." Marcie kisses Jack's cheek. "Come on honey."

Jack has a bottle of Jack Daniels under his arm. He looks at me blankly, like he's trying to place me. Then he extends a hand to me. "Nice to be here finally."

As I return the handshake, Jack tilts his head to the side a little, with that dazzling smile. He must have his teeth whitened professionally. His hair is too long, the true sign of a vain dick. And the silver bracelet is just the capper.

Marcie and he walk away whispering. Candy observes, "She's already bitching to him about the house."

"Look, you know Marcie's going to have a problem with this place."

Candy sighs. "And leave it to you, Richard, to be the one to remind me."

"What?" I freeze, my hands in the air. I hate it when she does the "Poor me" thing.

"You people are never happy, no matter how hard I try." Candy shakes her head, gathering plates, glasses and napkins from the table, exhaling loudly. I want to say, "Don't act like such a martyr," but I don't.

A skirmish erupts in the living room. I hear Austin scream with rage at his sister, Madison. Candy shakes her head. More huffing and puffing and sighing. "I'll break it up."

The screen door slams behind her and all my muscles go slack, as I lean back, sip my beer and notice the seagulls patrolling the horizon.

Thank God Marcie didn't hear me when I said I'm thinking of leaving Candy. Telling Marcie a secret is like putting it on the radio. What was I thinking?

I'm also grateful for Marcie's diplomacy tonight over these crummy rental houses. But if I know my sister, Marce ain't gonna be able to keep quiet for long. Me? Why I've been biting my tongue so long there's a hole in it.

Why do we vacation with these people? I don't get it. The women just complain. They complain about the kids, the husbands, the parent teacher association, the schools, the teachers, the scout troop leader, you name it. They complain endlessly and insist they're right. Their indignity and righteousness is the subtext under every conversation.

Oh and how the women betray each other! Complaining about each other behind each other's backs! *She doesn't watch her kids! She never opens her wallet! She wanted to feed the kids Lunchables!* And it's all a guy can do to find a place to get away from all the complaining.

Who was that woman entering the water this afternoon? That gigantic, obese woman, coming toward me, in slow motion, calling to me, waving? For a long, long moment, I didn't know who that woman was. Sun and salt water in my eyes, yes, but it was the *size* of her silhouette that bewildered me. *Who's this? Is she talking to me?* And then I realized that obese woman was Candy. My wife. And I just had to turn away, dive into the water, my forehead breaking the wave, breaking away, swimming under water, away from that gigantic woman who I did not marry. My forehead hit the wave, BOOM! My thoughts exploded. Like a door shutting inside my head, BOOM! The closing of a door behind me, BOOM! I surfaced and kept swimming, away from that fat lady. *BOOM slammed the door in my head.*

Right now, Candy is behind the screen door, lumbering inside the house. I can hear the floorboards bend beneath her. But here, behind the door, I'm away from the fat lady. I don't have to pretend. My mind drifts with the seagulls. The moon is massive, washed in gold. And in front of the big rock, the rising waves reach around and swirl together.

I'm thinking about leaving Candy, I almost said it.

Not loud enough, but I began to say it. That's a start.

I wonder when I'll say it loudly enough to be heard?

I feel my blood race in my forearms, like I'm running away from home, like the beginning of an adventure, like escape from Alkatraz!

I'm thinking about leaving Candy.

I look across the walkway to the house on the left. Tall and newly shingled, surrounded by wild beach plums and neat paved stone walkways. Is that a cupola on top? It's dark over there on the front porch. I wonder if anyone's renting it this week? One pinkish light on upstairs.

I think I maybe hear the murmur of low conversation. It sounds a little sexy. Candy and the kids are yelling in the background, so it's hard to hear.

I kind of reposition myself and squint to see what's going on across the way. The moon brightens. On the front porch, I see the barest outlines of two people in a hammock. The hammock swings slightly. I realize I'm looking at two naked people and one is a woman and she is smokin' hot.

I don't move. They might catch me in this act of voyeurism. But shit, she's laying on top of her man, her back against his chest, her front fully exposed to the moonlight. My eyes adjust. Her breasts and pussy are pale. Tan lines. Whoa. My cock jumps.

I think he's giving it to her from behind. He's got his hands under her tits, which are the size of bicycle helmets, *naw, more like footballs,* his thumbs rubbing her nipples. She's bushless, and I can see her wide-open pussy as she caresses her clit with sparkly long fingernails.

My boner is immediate. I can't move. I can't drink my beer. I can't avert my eyes. Can't do anything but watch this goddess, her lips opening and closing, like she gives the best head on the planet, as she pleasures herself. He's giving it to her from behind all right. Her nipples are like darts as he only holds her breasts from beneath. He teases her. His thumbs play, she silently gasps and arches. Now he takes over pussy duty and she caresses her own breasts. I'm rock hard. Throbbing.

The Goddess whispers, *"Ohhh, holy dooley!"* She's breathing, moaning, as his fingers rub her button counterclockwise. She speaks with some kind of foreign accent. My mouth is hanging open, my cock is like Mount Saint Helen's, as he brings her off, and she arches gloriously, repeatedly, her breasts heaving, "Uh! Ohhhhhh . . . . Uhhhhhhh . . . . Ohhhhhhh . . . ." her pussy thrusting and contracting, reaching, and he's giving it to her, he's coming too, I hear him. They're both coming and now I'm coming too. I feel the sudden rush. The release, shooting out into my boxers.

Oh God that felt good. My head drops back, my breath stabilizes.

But this is weird. I feel like I've flown to the moon and back. And yet, The Fat Lady and kids are in the house, behind the door. I lean back a little bit, still watching.

The mystery couple lay there, collapsed, panting, and then, The Goddess laughs. She laughs and laughs and laughs like cathedral bells. Such joyous, musical, contagious laughter, she throws her head back, her hair flowing, her mouth wide open, teeth flashing, eyes alight.

She slides out of the hammock, thump, her feet hit the porch with the agility of a cat. I see the outline of her ass and curved back, long hair over her shoulders. Not an ounce of fat on her. She turns and runs into the house. Her tall, hairy ape man pads after her.

I take the tray of snacks and put it over my stained lap. Just then, Candy sticks her head through the screen door, "I'm putting the kids to bed. Want some ice cream? On a brownie? With whipped cream?"

"No thanks." It's then that I remember, I haven't had sex in five years.

6 It's Too Darn Hot

Marcie was right. The rental house is a real shit hole. It is not worth three thousand dollars a week—they should be paying *me* three thousand dollars a week to stay here.

And I don't give a fuck that it's on Candy's favorite lousy beach. I can't make a goddamn phone call. I can't send a goddamn email! Has no one heard of WIFI?

The whole place drones with goddamn flies, screens full of holes. There's no air conditioner, no ice maker, no overhead fans, no dishwasher. No washer, no nothing.

So the kids are asleep across the hall. Up in the bedroom, I'm drinking lukewarm Jack Daniels. A mosquito whines around my ear. It's like boiler room in here. We have this cheap little plastic fan pointed at us. And Marcie starts to go down on me. Her tongue circles the tip of my limp cock.

"Oh honey. It's too hot."

I try to coax her away but she takes me all the way in. Her mouth full, she laughs. I shift my pelvis, sliding my exhausted cock from her mouth. Marcie glances up, her eyes predatory, her hair all wild and sexy around her face.

"Jack. Come on! You'll feel better."

"Only air conditioning can make me feel better!"

"Come on." She's insistent. "I want sex."

"Not now! Not here. I'm miserable! Please Marcie. *Cut it out!*"

She backs off when she hears my Asshole Tone. My Asshole Tone works on Marcie. On all women, actually. "What is that fucking realtor's number?"

"Candy has it." Marcie has rolled over and lays wide open in the white sheets. Her little shaved pussy and tits are white, the rest of her tennis-tight body is a nice toasted shade. She is very hot, and I kind of want to stick my fingers in her, but I'm spent.

"How about tomorrow morning, when we wake up, if I ever get to goddamn sleep that is?" I grin. I know this will never happen because we'll have kids all over us in the morning.

"Whatever you say, Jack. Just need to be fucked and soon." She turns on her side, and yawns. This is why I like Marcie. She follows orders. Not a lot of flack. I trained her well.

"Don't you worry Marce. I'm getting that number from Candy and I'm going to kick that realtor's ass. I'm going to rip her a new one."

"Look, Jack. If you're not going to fuck me then let me sleep. Cut the chit-chat."

"Well okay."

I'm Lord of the Flies here, I think. One is a horse fly, I discover as the sonofabitch bites the inside of my ankle. *That's it!* I get out of bed, my feet slide on the sandy floor. I look in on the twins and Jack Junior. Despite flies circling overhead, they're sleeping away, that evasive deep sleep children enjoy.

This sucks.

I tip-toe down stairs. Don't know why I bother tip toeing. The stairs creak like an old pier. I pour myself another glass of warm Jack. I walk over to the TV, circa 1982, some kind of huge honking Sony Trinitron. I click on the remote and then the worst thing, the very worst aspect of his shit hole is revealed to me. It's a fucking black and white TV. With cable. They have fucking cable on a black and white TV! With cable! This is insanity!

I'm going to rip that realtor a new one.

Why we have to vacation with Marcie's brother and The Whale, I'll never know. *Why?* Even their kids are fat. I mean, everything with them is eating. *Do you want some chips? How about some cake?* That bitch is a fucking food pimp. One thing for sure, that bastard Richard isn't getting any. You can tell.

All I want is a fucking ice cube! I open this tiny fucking refrigerator and there isn't even freezer burn in the upper compartment. The fucking thing isn't even functional. Why the Christ didn't Marcie call me and tell me to bring some fucking ice? Oh right. *There's no fucking cell phone reception, that's why!*

What are we doing here?

The floors are the cheapest stick-on linoleum you can buy. Might as well have used contact paper. Everything's sticky and sandy. The soles of my feet are gunky with God knows what, flies are hitting the screens, trying to escape this hell. I open a closet, and find fifty fly swatters hanging from rusty nails. *Now, what does that tell you?*

I grab a cigar and go out on the porch. The temperature drops like fifty degrees. It is a hundred percent better out here. I sit down and yes indeed, there are big rocks for the kids to climb on. More like big rocks for the kids to break their necks on. I cut my cigar and light it. I only feel about twenty-five percent better than I did before. But still, that's an improvement.

I think about Gwen, stretched across the bed at The Pierre. I think about giving it to her up the ass. She didn't like it at first, it hurt and she cried out loud, but I pushed in and when she got used to it, she liked it. Gwen has the most beautiful, tight ass. Marcie has a nice ass, but it's not a cello ass. Marcie's ass is a tennis ass. A tight little tennis ass. And I'm grateful for it. I'm grateful that she's not like The Fucking Whale next door. You'd need a goddamn crane to fuck Candy. But Marcie does the pilates and all that shit so she's got a nice 35-year-old ass. But still. Nobody beats Gwen. Pussy, in its twenties, is at the height of its sexiness. Gwen's pussy is as lush as a peony, her ass as rounded as a cello, as rich as a Carravagio painting.

So I'm sitting, I'm looking out at the water. It's nice. But it would be so much nicer from a house with finished floors, windows from this decade, central air, working appliances, more than one bathroom. Well I'm gonna rip that realtor a new one tomorrow.

Some clouds float past the moon, setting the waterline horizon alight. And I take another drink because I think I'm hallucinating, but there's a naked woman out there skinny-dipping. This caveman dude is watching her from the shore. He's wearing shorts. But she's buck ass naked and she is hot. A ten. Maybe an eleven. I'd say she might even be sexier than Gwen. Long wet hair, long legs, narrow hips. Round ass, two scoops. The tits are real. And big. I'm sitting there, watching this mythological creature emerge from the water, she's soaking wet and drenched in silver moonlight. She walks out of the water and the dude just stands there. *Fuck her, you moron!*

Get this. She kneels in front of him, pulls out his woodie and takes him into her mouth, her breasts swinging. I'm getting hard, but let's face it, after the weekend I've had, I'm kind of worn out . . . but always *interested!*

Just then, headlights from a car above the sea wall rapidly trace the waterline. He strokes her hair, says something to her and she releases his cock from her lips, gets up, stands. They realize the headlights are going to catch them, so they run, laughing, splashing. She's running naked across the beach, tits flying, around the rock, and they're headed right this way. Holy shit. I tamp out my cigar. I pull myself into shadow and stay perfectly still.

Holy fuck! *They're staying in the house on the other side of Richard and The Whale.* I watch this chick go up the stairs. Slinky precision. I could encircle her waist with one hand. Nothing shakes but her tits. In my head, I can hear The Knack playing "My Sharona." She's had a Brazilian waxing. She's pure pussy and real tits. My kind of girl. The diameter of her nipples, everything about her is Playboy perfect. She and the dude disappear in the house.

I sit there. In shock. Pour myself more Jack and finish my cigar, hoping my dick will go to sleep. Wow. Maybe staying here isn't so bad?

7   Welcome To The Neighborhood

Richard and the kids are still asleep even though it's nine. The coffee is brewing and I'm baking cinnamon rolls. I set the timer and walk to the window. *There is my beach!* The sheer happiness of being here thrills me. I haven't felt this happy in so long.

This is my favorite place in the world. And being here, the morning light on Miner's Rock . . . Elephant Rock is gleaming red, the tide glossing every surface, revealing the little inlet where we used to catch shellfish when we were kids. The seagulls squawk and the ocean rolls along, lulling my soul. Everything sparkles.

There's no one out there yet, so I pour coffee and step out to the porch. I'm in my bathrobe, but who cares? Seagulls are trolling the water's edge for clams. Maybe we should have steamers tonight?

Although I must admit, I love the drawn butter, I also love the ritual of steamers and lobsters. Everyone sitting together, opening the shells, peeling out the meat, dipping in the water, dipping in the butter, dropping the buttered seafood in the mouth, then tossing the shells into a bowl. I even love the bibs! I brought a dozen! They were six for a dollar at The Christmas Tree Shop.

The timer rings and the fragrance of baked cinnamon overtakes the house. The rolls slide onto my favorite tray. It's from Crate & Barrel and I brought it because it has little lobsters on it. I use my Williams & Sonoma pastry brush to coat the rolls with sugar. I decide to put out the butter dish, so the butter can be nice and soft. This butter dish I bought at Wal Mart. It's plastic and has a snap-on cover. It just makes sense for a week on the beach, you know?

I return to my chores on the porch. A bowl of damp Doritoes entertains tiny black flies. Picking it up, turning to the screen door, I hear snoring. I turn to the right, look over to Marcie's porch, and there is Jack, passed out in a deck chair, cigar in hand, mouth wide open. I stifle a laugh and smile.

I rarely get the opportunity to look at Jack. Whether it's Thanksgiving or Easter, he never stands still long enough to have a real conversation. Perpetually on the phone, texting, checking email. Or in his car, driving to FedEx, golf courses, liquor stores and airports. Always one foot out the door. Even at Easter dinner, he's heading around the buffet table, getting another beer, going out to the car to get his jacket, sliding out the door for basketball in the driveway with the boys. Aside from only the most marginal conversational ("Do you have a fax machine?") and social necessities ("What grade is Austin in?") I'm nothing more to Jack than the fat lady who's blocking TV screen.

Jack's face, so boyish yet craggy and unshaven, with dimples and a snub of a nose, is handsome. His crow's feet don't age him. He snores like a railroad train. Poor Marcie. His head drops to his chest and he instinctively rights it, snuffling and breathing. I notice Mr. Jack has a big "pup tent" happening in his shorts. He also has sleep apnea, I realize. You can have surgery for that. I should mention that to Marcie. I zip into the living room, grab my camera and without waking him, I snap a photo. I feel a sense of empowerment. I have a photo of Jack asleep, mid-cigar, snoring away with a hard-on. Very handy for a silly birthday card, I giggle to myself.

Of course, Jack would be enraged to see this picture. He's very image conscious. I guess you have to be, being a big-shot intellectual property attorney in New York.

I'm the opposite. Richard and I care less about image. We understand the realities of life and marriage. Not like Jack and Marcie. They always have the latest and the greatest and all designer labels, dontcha know. That's why Marcie's mad about these rental houses. She can't brag to her friends about how magnificent her vacation was.

Jack must have sensed me staring at him. He startles awake. He blinks a lot, sits up, turns his face to the ocean and barks, "What time is it?"

"Good morning Jack! It's nine." I smile. He looks bewildered. "It's me! Candy! How about some coffee and a cinnamon roll? I just baked them!" He blinks across the porch railing at me. Shakes his head like a dog.

"How about a Coke and a meat ball sub?" He stands, chuckles, yawns loudly and stretches. "Candy? What I *would* like is to call that incompetent bitch at the realtors office."

I was just about to go into the house to grab him a can of Coke from our fridge. But something stops me when Jack approaches the porch railing and I see his expression. Like he's just had diarrhea.

"What?"

"Listen. Candy. This rental house is really—and I hate to say this but—it's really crappy." His smile is not a nice one.

I tip my head to the side and smile. "Thanks, Jack, I think?"

"I'm saying, time for you to wake up and drink that coffee you got there." He motions the stub of his cigar to my coffee mug.

"What's your issue Jack?" I refuse to let Jack and Marcie ruin this for me. They didn't lift a computer mouse to search for our vacation rentals, so they're just as much at fault as I am.

"What's my issue? *My issue?*" Jack's voice has a razor edge, a threatening tone.

"Stop it."

"Candy. I'm sorry to rain on your parade. But I am not paying three thousand dollars for this shack. They should be paying me!"

"It is what it is Jack."

"I need a working refigerator. I need central air."

"Geeze, Jack. Man up."

"Three thousand bucks for this?"

"Why make a fuss? You can rough it for a week."

He relights the butt of his cigar, gesturing with his other hand. "Gimme the lease."

"I don't have it!" I feel my face redden, sweat explodes from every pore.

Jack freezes with a look that radios my incompetence to the world. "Give me the phone number."

I fold my arms. "Listen Jack. I really like the realtor, Mrs. Ross."

"Give me the fucking phone number!" He sucks on his cigar butt, turns and yells into the window, like a child, "Marcie, Candy won't give me the Realtor's number!"

"Quiet down!" Marcie enters the porch, wearing a chic teal cover-up. She has her Kate Spade bag and Chanel sunglasses. She dots her lips with Blistex as she checks her iPhone. "Still no reception."

"Look you guys, if I'd known you wanted the Taj Mahal—" I sigh.

"Not the Taj Mahal, Marcie, but not a youth hostel!"

Where's Richard when I need someone to back me up? Gone, of course.

Marcie thinks for a minute. "I'm just going to ask the Realtor about other houses."

"Don't embarrass me?"

"Look Candy, that woman took advantage of you."

"That bitch must be getting a decent cut of that $3,000 for pimping out this crackhouse . . ." Jack blusters, champing his cigar.

"I'll say we want our money refunded and we want to stay at the Wintusket Harbor Inn."

"That's my girl!" Jack slaps Marcie's ass. She smiles.

I go to sip my coffee and find a dead bug floating on the surface. "Marcie, just so you know, The Inn is sold out. There's a big wedding in town."

Marcie puts her phone in her bag and snarls, "Well I've got to do something Candy because this is just unacceptable. Okay?" Her heels click down the steps.

I snap back. "Whatever." Just then, the kids and Richard stumble out onto the porch in their swimsuits. The kids run straight to the water, Richard about to follow. "What?" he asks.

"Nothing." I call after the kids, "Would anyone like a cinnamon roll? Lucky Charms?"

Austin dives into a shallow wave and Madison skips over it.

"I'll have coffee," Richard asks as he buckles his Tevas. He looks exhausted. One eyebrow is askew and a lock of his dark gray hair sticks up. He's not looking me in the eye.

"Coming right up," It's a relief to escape Marcie and Jack. In the kitchen, I pour Richard's coffee and sneak a cinnamon bun when no one's looking. From the window above the kitchen stove, I study the terse body language of Marcie and Jack as they shout at each other in front of her extra-long white Escalade, tacky, trimmed in gold. The way Jack points, Marcie's fists on her hips, all indicate more bad news on the horizon. They gesture to Richard, who tiredly hands Marcie the realtor's card.

8   This Land Is My Land

Okay get this. I'm standing out in the middle of the road, trying to get some decent phone reception. My iPhone wavers. The signal display shrinks.

I'm walking further and further from the house when finally I hear, "Wintusket Realty! May I help you?"

"Yes, Betty Ross, please."

I get that contrived tone of an unreceptive receptionist. "She's not here right now. May I connect you with her voice mail?"

"Okay, but first, can you take a message?"

"No I can't. I'm connecting you to her direct line, Ma'am."

Oh, how I hate to be called ma'am.

What a little bitch. I get the recording and the beep. I say, "Hi. This is Marcie White. I understand you're a friend of my sister in law's—Candy Grant—and I just want to speak with you. We're renting Red Rock Cottage and upon arriving, the house is unacceptable, so we need to discuss alternatives right away. Thanks."

As I cross the road and head back to the houses, a bent old woman hobbles towards me. "You! You! Stop!"

"Me?" She wobbles over, reaching like she's about to fall, so I extend my arm. Stooped over a driftwood stick, her fingers reach up, her cold hand imprints my bicep. Her face, drawn as tightly as the tie end of a balloon, closes in on me. "Are you the one who left that kayak in my front yard?"

I speak slowly and loudly, "You must be confused ma'am. We're renting Red Rock Cottage and yes, our kayak is in front of our cottage, yes and that's okay."

The old woman, wearing a cheap nightgown and worn terry cloth slippers, points a yellow-nailed finger at me, "I'm not confused. That is my land! My rock, my ocean, my land!"

I can see her pink skull beneath a froth of white hair. She smells like pee.

"Yes I'm sure it is. But we're renting that house and it's okay. Don't worry!" I smile soothingly.

Her eyes are fierce. "No it's not okay! That's my land! Get that thing off my land?"

Clearly crazy, I get the heck outta there. Palm to my ear, I formulate my escape. "Oops! I hear my twins. Gotta run!"

Then I hustle around the corner, up the steps of Beach Rock Cottage. Jack and Richard are turned to the water, hands in pockets. "I left a message," I declare to Richard and slide the business card into his shirt pocket. "Betty's not in the office, so there's no point in driving over there."

"Good for you," Jack mumbles.

"Where are the kids? I ask Richard and Jack. Trancelike, they stare straight ahead. "Jack? Where are the kids?"

"They're playing down there, under the porch." Jack doesn't move.

Richard mutters, "They say they like the shade."

"Listen you guys, there's this crazy old lady wandering around out back." Jack stares straight ahead. "That's nice."

Two minutes ago he was screaming at me and now he's hypnotized by the view. Richard, too.

"Think she might have escaped from a nursing home? Think I should call the police?"

No answer. They stare ahead. I squint to see what they're looking at, then the kids come flying out from under the porch, squealing.

Austin and Jack Junior race each other, Austin's stomach shakes like a water balloon as he tries to keep up with Jack Junior. I see the twins and Madison begin the makings of a hole, they seem fine, so I go inside for coffee.

"I like Madison's bathing suit."

"Old Navy. Five bucks." Candy grins.

"She's a funny little shape, isn't she?" The minute I say it, I wish I hadn't. Truth is, Madison is fat.

"Oh Madison will shoot up. She's going to be tall like me." Candy nods, confident that Madison will stretch out, but I'm not so sure. In the kitchen, flies perform aeronautics over buns, blackberries, and juice. The room is a blast furnace.

"Just so you know Candy, I left a message with the realtor. She wasn't in the office." She ignores me, folding beach towels.

"Listen Candy, I know you love this beach. But if Jack and I had known about the condition of these—accommodations, I never would have agreed."

"Oh geeze Marcie will ya cut it out?" Candy's squeezes her eyes, as though I'm missing the point, which I'm not.

"It's not that bad. Make yourself a plate and relax will ya!"

This is just like Candy, thinking everything can be solved with a buffet. "Try to have fun. Will you?"

Candy throws a blackberry into her mouth.

"I can't relax when we're so completely being ripped-off! I mean, our house doesn't even have ice!"

"So we'll go buy some ice! Put it in the cooler!"

"Three thousand dollars a week? No icemaker?"

"Are you telling me Jack can't afford it? Look. It's a week without the luxuries. So what?"

"Ice is not a luxury."

"Look. The kids are having a great time. They don't care. You'd feel better if you eat."

"No, I don't want anything except to get the hell out of here. Come on Candy! Jack is not happy."

Candy looks amused. "Really? Jack looks pretty happy right now."

I look out the window. The men couldn't be more relaxed, watching the waves, the horizon.

"Will ya look that that."

Candy pulls her black hair into a scrunchie ponytail. "If you ask me, Jack's probably a little hungover. That Jack Daniels bottle is half full."

Candy looks at me pointedly.

Oh so Candy's watching what we *drink?* Someone should be watching what *she eats!* I add, "Don't be a cocktail Nazi Candy. This is vacation."

Candy mimics a baby, "Oh Jack isn't happy. Poor Jack. Things aren't perfect for Jack, boo hoo."

I can't help but giggle at Candy's spot-on imitation of Jack. "You're mocking us."

Candy puts cantaloupe slices on a bright tray and covers it with Saran Wrap. "I'm happy to be here. If you want to leave, leave. Just please don't insult the realtor. Obviously she wasn't entirely truthful on the conditions here, but what the heck? We're here. The kids are happy. We'll adjust. We'll have fun. I brought Scrabble!"

"Oh listen, there's this crazy old lady out there, wandering around. She told me this is her land. And she wants our kayak off her beach."

"That's crazy."

"Maybe she escaped from a nursing home. She was in her pajamas."

"Hmmm. That's strange."

"Should I call the police, just to give them an FY!?"

"No, no, no. Maybe she'll go away."

9 Feel the Heat

I'm a fool. This is no vacation. I'm like the unpaid hired help. I'm making breakfast, serving coffee. I'm on the road, getting ice, bug spray and citronella candles. I'm in the kitchen, sweat pouring into my eyes. Just because I made the mistake of signing the lease, I'm the go-to girl for any request. "Ask Aunt Candy," is the answer.

At least the kids are happy. They run everywhere. They run to the water. They run with buckets filled with water. They run to a sand castle. They run back and forth between the houses. I can't tell you how happy I feel seeing the kids out running on the beach and watching the twins nap on the sofa. Long eyelashes, pink cheeks, bouquets of curls across the pillows. Looking out the windows, I love seeing Richard and Jack sitting together. Marcie sits with them, but I can't see her face. But she looks mad. Of course.

Ah, the woman who has everything is never happy.

I see that Richard's chest and nose are really getting sunburned.

What's he thinking?

I marinate two pounds of fresh blue fish in savingnon blanc, soy sauce and lemon juice. I add some peppercorns. Then I add some capers. Thinking ahead, I had brought my Williams Sonoma grilling pan, perfect for fish. I set up the gas grill on the far end of the porch. The afternoon shadows grow long.

After naps, trips to the ice cream truck and attempts to revive expiring crustaceans, I order the kids to gather driftwood for a fire. I carry out the coffee table from the house, and set it with bowls, napkins and bibs. The butter is ready. The fish is marinated. The steamers are clean. The lobsters flail anxiously in a brown paper bag. I even brought my stainless steel double boiler. The sun is cooperating, the curve of a distant peninsula glimmers.

Richard tends the fire as the boys play paddleball and the girls splash in the water. Marcie helps me. We've always been a great team when serving a meal. The steamers open like flowers to eager hands that strip and dip them in drawn butter. I set out the grilled bluefish, both Richard and Jack squeeze lemon wedges over the squares of sizzling fish. The lobsters come next. The kids are fascinated as their fathers demonstrate how to pull lobsters apart. But the kids stick with their hotdogs. The moon rises, and as I serve a cold Key Lime pie and lemon ice cream cones, two scrawny, tanned children join us.

'Good day . . . Mind if we join yuz?" *They're Australian!* Right behind them, there appears a beautiful woman, wearing a white sundress. Even in this low light, I can see the darkness of her nipples beneath the fabric's gauziness. She stands with her pelvis thrust forward.

"Mind if we join you!" Her grin reveals a gap between her front teeth.

"No! Please! Sit down!" Richard and Jack couldn't be more accommodating. Richard offers her beach chair, but she refuses and sits on the sand.

"Hi! I am Giselle." She grins, the gap makes her look slightly vulgar.

I don't extend a hand as I scoop lemon sorbet. "I'm Candy!"

She sits Indian style while the campfire flickers, her two little ones cling behind. I don't like her open legs. She's not very lady like. Richard seems to redden even further as Jack holds Jack Junior on his lap, sharing the ice cream cone.

I pull the attention away from her. "Marshmallows everyone!"

The kids scream with delight. "Sticks!" Madison cries and gleefully takes off. The Australian kids race along to find sticks. Jack and Richard pretend to not look at the woman.

Marcie hollers after them, "Hey, Hailey, that's not a stick!"

I add, "Austin, that's a feather! Put it down!"

Marcie glares at the Australian woman and asks tightly, "So what brings you here?"

Then it hits me. The reason why Jack has stopped complaining about the house and the reason why Richard sat in the sun for nine hours—the reason is *this woman.*

Observation: At Miner's Beach, proper beach etiquette means:

No radios, unless the radio is tuned to a Red Sox game.

One does not bring anything more than a bag and a low beach chair.

Inside the bag you will find a pair of sunglasses, a book, a towel, water bottles and money

for the ice cream truck.

Sun block is applied at home, before leaving for the beach.

Children are permitted one bucket and one shovel. Nothing more is needed.

One does not untie the back of one's bikini top when reclining on one's stomach.

Faux pas, faux pas, faux pas.

10 The Girl Can't Help It

Okay, so Jack is suddenly fine with staying in the flea bitten, horse fly ridden hell hole of Red Rock Cottage. And I know why he's changed his mind. I saw that woman. She may be Australian, but she's no idiot. She sun bathed, all day wearing a thong. Getting away from sights like that on the Jersey Shore was one reason why I agreed to come here.

I don't know about Richard, but I knew right then that Jack was glued to the spot. Which meant I wasn't going anywhere. No chat with the realtor. No drive to town.

I had a look at that body. Perfect. Pilates, yoga, personal trainer, full body massages. Major bikini waxing. Her eyebrows, lip and legs were waxed. The upper lip may have gotten a nice boost of silicone. Her long hair has been chemically straightened with blonde highlights. Eyelash extensions. Maybe a spray tan. Some serious monthly maintenance money goes into looking that way.

I know because *I have all of that too!* I have not had a piece of bread for two years. I've given up coffee, soda, sugar, rice and potatoes. I work out every single day. But I will never have a body like that.

And I will never wear tacky nail polish like that. Glitter. As if she doesn't attract enough attention already, she is compelled to wear silver glitter nail polish?

And another thing. If you want nude sunbathing, go to a nude beach. Go to a clothing optional resort. But for Christ's sake—*there are children here! There are husbands here!* When Jack Jr. got a look at her, he yelled, *"Mom! That lady isn't wearing any pants!"*

That's when I went to complain about indecent exposure to the lifeguards, three teenage guys, who all were about to burst out laughing in my face. They told me there wasn't anything they could do. I heard them snickering as I walked away. I went out into the road to call the police but couldn't get a signal.

What really kills me is, Candy was oblivious to it all! And Richard was looking at that Australian, believe me! Every male on the beach was panting! This incredibly beautiful woman had her top untied—the sides of her huge breasts pressed against the sand, and her perfect ass, every crack and crevice—totally revealed to the world.

"This ain't Australia," I felt like yelling.

Instead of paying attention to her husband, Candy spent the whole day in the kitchen or riding off in her minivan. She was cooking and messing around in that hot house, baking and marinating, and she had no idea that our men spent the entire day staring at—for all intents and purposes—a naked woman.

Worse, I had to sit there, pretending like it didn't matter. I had to sit there to prevent my husband from simply unzipping his cock and fucking her on the beach. Her long legs. Perfect ass. No cellulite. None. Her super large boobs, which let me tell you, *are so fake*, were driving men to dive into the water. But the worst part of all of this is, the thing that really kills me is—she's like, my age.

Ah, but there is a happy ending.

That weird old lady? In the pajamas? The kook with the cane? She appears by our kayak, struggling and shaking, and she starts hitting our kayak with her cane. "Get this thing out of here!" she yells.

Jack and the kids leap up and run over. Calmly, unleashing his killer smile, Jack says, "Hey, hey! Ma'am. Calm down, calm down. Now what's the problem?"

Shuffling in her slippers, she hits the kayak again. "Get this out of here. Now!"

"Hey! Wait! You'll put a hole in it!" Jack catches the end of her cane in his hand, which infuriates her. She attempts to pull it away, shouting "Let go! Let go right now!"

Everyone has turned their attention from the nudist to the Red Rock Cottage confrontation, as Jack tries to talk the old lady down. "Listen. We're renting this house! It's perfectly okay to keep the kayak here."

The old lady narrows her eyes. "That is my house and this is my land. No boats allowed. It's in the lease!"

"Really? Well we didn't know that." Jack coaxes her with, "Can we move it to our car?"

"I don't care if you move it to Poughkeepsie, just get it the hell out of my yard." She sort of teeters on her feet for a second as she looks around the beach. The old bat realizes that everyone is staring at her. Suddenly, she stops. Her eyes may be mottled, but they're sharp. She is staring at The Bottom. "What the hell!" she shouts and starts heading toward the Butt. "You*! You!*"

Giselle rolls over, holds her bikini top to her breasts. "Moi?"

Old Lady, whom I now admire wholeheartedly, hits Butt's water bottle with her stick and declares war on Australia.

"You get some decent clothing on or get the hell off my beach."

"What, ya old knocker?" Giselle's thick Australian slang cheapens her even more than the glitter nail polish. The old lady waves her stick, the Aussie turns to avoid getting hit, and reveals more of her right breast. The men suck in their collective breath.

Growling, Old Lady closes in. "Harlot! You have a jewel in your naval? You're a disgrace! Get off my beach! Get off my land!"

"All right! You don't have to lair it up!" Giselle's face, a study in brave humiliation. The Old Lady stands over her, threatening.

"You're a *disgrace!*"

Giselle fights to tie the back of her bikini top, as the Old Lady's cane tips up a towel from the sand and hurls it over Giselle's ass. She's quite deft. The lifeguards howl, as a discombobulated Giselle scrambles to cover herself and get out of there.

Richard's face is frozen in disappointment.

"This is my land!" the Old Lady declares to the world, as Jack and the kids carry the kayak to my mini-van.

Victory over Australia.

11 The Show's Over

I was disappointed after the Old Lady's meltdown. I must admit, I loved looking at that ass. Firm and round, tanned and glowing, the polar opposite of Candy's gigantic cauliflower rear.

I've long since lost the way and the will to navigate those folds. It's been years since I've watched my wife undress.

Candy chose bacon sandwiches and cookies over me, long ago. So I rationalize, it's my right to indulge in this newfound, live erotica on Miner's Beach. And now, this schitzo Old Woman ended it. I feel robbed. I turn toward the house. I figure, I'll pour myself a giant vodka and jack off in that rusty old shower.

But no. The Old Lady wretches and calls to me, "You! You! Yes you! Is she one of your people? *You sir!* Is that your woman?"

My fantasy of cold vodka and ejaculation go poof! "Me? Are you talking to me?"

"Yes you!" Why isn't she having a stroke or a heart attack in this heat?

"Uh, no. She's not—"

"I am Mrs. Briggs!"

Trying to be polite, "Hi. I'm Richard Grant. I'm renting Beach Rock Cottage."

"That's my cottage! My land!" Her blue eyes emerge from a face gathered with a multitude of wrinkles and brown spots, hairs and lines.

"This is your land?" Oh God. That's all I need now is this kook.

"Darn tootin' it is." She plants her cane like a flag.

"But I thought—" I was going to say, this is public land, but she plows right in.

"I'm gonna tell you something, young man."

She cuts in front, leaving me mumbling in her path. "Uh, uh, but I'm not sure I . . ."

"Right this way." So I fall in, up the steps, she ignores the children, lolling with popsicles on the front porch. Mrs. Briggs walks right through the screen door, blows past Candy, doesn't hear Candy's curt "can I help you?" and shuffles her way with surprising agility to the far wall of the living room. "Do you see this picture young man?" The tip of her cane shakily indicates a framed sepia tone photograph. "Uhhhh. Yes I do. Yes, ma'am."

"See that lady? That's my mother."

"Really?"

"Yes really. My uncle." As I zoom in, I realize it's an original Daguerreotype of Miner's Beach. Back then, Miner's Rock had a heavy wooden staircase bolted onto its side. A haughty looking woman in full skirts, holding her shawl and parasol stood regally on top of the rock. From the sand, a man with a full handlebar moustache, wearing a bowler hat, vest, knickers and a bow tie stood, proudly holding the reins of a glossy horse.

"Wow." I nod appreciatively. "So your family goes that far back?"

"And they're rolling in their graves over that unspeakable display today!"

"That's nothing compared to the Jersey Shore," Candy tosses out, smiling.

Mrs. Briggs, examines Candy warily, "You tell that friend of yours she's not permitted to—"

Candy squeezes her eyes in confusion, "What friend?"

I chuckle, "Ma'am, we have nothing to do with that woman. She's renting the house across the way."

"Oh." Mrs. Briggs is disappointed. "The Curtis House. That's not one of mine."

Candy comes swooping over with a tray, "Iced tea. Nice and cold."

"Well all right." Mrs. Briggs reluctantly sits, her lips tremble around the straw. Candy squeezes into the settee.

"I'm Candy Grant. This is my husband, Richard. We're from New Jersey, but I summered right here in town. A few years back that is, heh-heh."

Candy tries to build the bond with Mrs. Briggs, but the Old Lady won't have it. In her eyes, Candy is no Townie.

After a dramatic pause, she pronounces, like an author reading aloud, "I am Gloria Briggs. I was born in 1920. In this house. Right upstairs." My eyes shoot to the ceiling, weirdly horrified, wondering if the mattresses have been replaced since her delivery.

"I live with my son and his green card wife," fortified with an audience, she waxes dramatic, "over there, two doors down. She's one of those Obama people."

God damn. She's introduced so many conversational land mines, I retrench. "So, you say this is your beach?"

"I don't just say it, I know it!" she barks back.

Candy refills Gloria's glass, "So Mrs. Briggs, I'm curious . . ." Candy thinks Mrs. Briggs is full of shit. "I thought *the town* owned this beach."

"No no no no no no no no no. *I* own this beach, these cottages, Beach Rock Cottage right here and Red Rock Cottage."

"So you must know Betty Ross! She's the realtor who rented us these places!" Candy's speaking extra loud and slowly.

Gloria pulls her bathrobe tighter around her neck. "Of course I know Betty! You must think I'm a moron!"

Candy falls back, silenced. Mrs. Briggs shivers. How can she be cold, it's an inferno in here? We sit there. Wiry white hairs shoot from her upper lip, long gray hairs spiral from her neck and behind her ears. I think to myself, *some day Candy's going to have all that plus obesity.*

Candy attempts to make some inroads. "Yes well, Betty's very nice. In fact, we're going to call her. About *the window screens—? The flies?*"

Gloria's eyes flash and she slams the butt of her stick on the floor, growling, pointing eerily at Candy's astonished face. *"Wait! You must be the one! You* left my garden hose in a mess by the side of my house!" Her mouth contorts with accusation.

"Oh my!" Candy whispers. I blink.

Candy and I are caught off guard by the sudden change of subject and the acid tone. With an apologetic giggle, Candy answers, "Well yes, I was just rinsing out our cooler so naturally I—"

Gloria's stick slams the floor. "You used my garden hose and you left it in a big tangle!" Gloria Briggs jiggles her way to a standing position.

"I want that hose hanging on the hook just the way you found it. Right now! Get up!"

Rolling her eyes, Candy follows Mrs. Briggs out the door. "I'm sorry, but I didn't realize—"

"None of you people ever realize! It's like you've never been to the beach before!"

The screen door slams behind them. I grab the bottle of Svedka and race upstairs to the bathroom.

Observation: Miner's Beach Etiquette, 1829

No mules, dogs or gypsies allowed on the beach.

Ladies must wear hats and carry parasols at all times.

Gentlemen may remove hats when swimming.

Ladies are not permitted to swim.

Picnics are permitted on Saturdays only.

No children on Miner's Rock.

Do not enter The Mine.

12 Cherche La Femme

Okay. So I've gotta find the way to fuck her.

Oh, come on!

I *have to have that woman.* She's all I can think about! I want to come in her mouth. Maybe in the car. That would be the ultimate. My coming in her mouth in the Porsche.

Cherche la femme.

The kids are asleep, Marcie's asleep, I don't know how they can sleep in this fry pan, but everyone's snoring away, so I fill a red plastic cup with J.D. and ice from the cooler. I trim up a cigar, light it and go on my midnight beach walk. The tide is coming in, the moon overhead. I walk east. I see a campfire or two along the beach. Teenagers, getting drunk, making out. On I trudge, puffing on my cigar, pretending I'm not looking for her, when I hear, "Oh, it's that horny American!" A wave of male laughter follows, "We're all horny Americans."

Giselle is keeping company with a circle of wasted losers. So I join the campfire.

"Nice night," I nod, watching her. She's sitting cross legged, next to a poser in a pork pie hat, his arms covered in tattoos and those idiotic earrings that stretch out your earlobes. Pork pie hat! What a fool. Just 'cause some stupid dick movie star wears a pork pie hat and now we're all stuck dealing with loser wannabes walking around wearing pork pie hats.

The dude to her right is a meathead with piercings all over and a stupid thumb ring.

Giselle is wearing more clothing than usual. The old lady must've made an impression. Clothed, unclothed, she is the most gorgeous of all, golden in the firelight, eyes throwing sparks. Her hair is long and wild, ribbons of butterscotch and chocolate.

My dick is on alert. I attempt to talk him down, as I ask laughing Giselle if she'd like me to *walk her home?* Ah but not yet, she explains, a joint is being rolled and about to be smoked. So I wait. A multi-racial tattooed mess of a human being sucks and sucks, then passes the joint to her. She takes a long hit and while I'm horrified by the germs she must be taking in from the mouth of that trash, I'm glad. Nothing like a good hit of weed to get a woman addle-minded enough so you can fuck her in a car. She passes it to me. No thanks. I have to be on top of my game.

Giselle looks up at me then smiles crookedly, that gap in her teeth making me think of her mouth on mine. I want her now and I ain't got much time, so I say, "Hey! It's late. Isn't it time to get back *to your kids*, Giselle?"

It takes a moment for her to process, but she agrees, looking around at her new friends sadly, "Oh pig's arse!" and stands. Wobbles. I grab her arm and place an arm around her shoulder, getting a sneak peek at those unbridled tits. Despite the protests of the losers circle, I remind them, "She's a Mom! She must get back to her children!"

"Hey man, she's got a nanny . . . !"

"Good night . . . . !"

From this angle, I can only see the top of her head and those amazing tits swinging with her every step. My dick is rising to the occasion. I pull her over to my left side, so I'm walking along the water's edge, and she's on higher ground. My left arm drops to precisely where the elastic band of her panties *should* be . . . "You're not wearing panties!"

She laughs. "You're a naughty one, aren't you?"

She has Bambi eyes. The whites so white, the irises large, lashes long.

My hand drops to cup a handful of ass cheek, but she steps aside and elbows my rib. "Stop it!"

She steps away from me. I face her, my eyes narrowed with desire. "I can't help it. You're so hot."

"I thought you were walking me home to my children."

"I'm walking you to my car so I can fuck you." My left arm softly swipes across the scoops of her ass. She steps further away, laughing, low and gravelly. My dick is like a radar tower.

"No thanks." Her lips pout and purse. Deliciously erect, I watch her as she walks a bit ahead of me, until I look up and see Richard standing in front of Beach Rock Cottage, watching us.

13 Ships Pass In The Night

Jack's not exactly happy to see me.

"Couldn't sleep?" I ask, eyebrows raised, as he returns from his failed conquest, face resolute, jaw tight.

"Nope!" Jack looks past me, taking a pull of his drink with a tap of his cigar. "Nice night."

"Sure is!" I cock my head to the side, my false gaiety aggravating him further, "Time for bed!?"

"Yeah." He steams past.

"Sweet dreams!" I raise my cup of Svedka.

He stomps up the stairs of Red Rock Cottage, caught, but not *caught in the act.*

I think I see the outline of a container ship on the horizon. When I hear the slam of a screen door, I drop down, sitting in the cold sand, and I start to think. About my sister, mostly.

Watching the distant container ship slide by, I wonder what life must be like for Marcie.

She never has to worry about money. Ever. For as long as she lives. Unless of course, Jack becomes a heroin addict and blows everything. Highly unlikely, Jack's self-preservation skills are perhaps his greatest strength. Marcie and the kids will always live in a house fit for the Queen of England, with indoor and outdoor pools, water falls, hot tubs, Jacuzzis, duck ponds and enough fountains and waterworks to rival Sea World. In her gated community, she is surrounded by women like herself. Beautiful. Coiffed. Shrewd. And thin. With big fake breasts, so fake, you can see the ridge of the implants displayed by their plunging necklines.

As her brother, I suppose it's reassuring to know that Marcie will never have to work, although she'll be the first to tell you how hard she works. Scheduling is mostly what she does, or so Candy tells me. Marcie schedules house keepers, landscapers, contractors and decorators. Nothing is ever perfect in her palace. Granite counter tops must be replaced with marble. Walls must be torn down. And the children! They must take French now, or lose any potential of attending

Harvard. Marcie schedules tutors, pediatricians, orthodontists, drama coaches, babysitters and private instructors for everything from tap dancing to tuba.

Above all, Marcie takes care of herself and is always the most beautiful woman within sight. That is, except when The Goddess is around. Marcie is the wife most men would dream of having.

Everyone except Jack.

When Marcie first introduced me to Jack, I knew he was a player.

Marcie met Jack in a Cleveland bar during an Ohio State-Michigan game. He was older. In town on business, brokering a deal. Licensed cartoon characters for a new line of Procter and Gamble children's bubble baths.

Jack starting hitting on Marcie as she ordered a drink at the bar. She ended up beating him at darts. Over a two year period, by hook or by crook, Marcie reeled Jack in, although he fought it and thrashed every inch of the way.

The wedding was something out of *Town & Country*, but it was by no means happy. Somebody caught Jack in a hotel custodian's closet with one of the female bartenders a few days before the wedding. My parents, God rest their souls, were prepared to kill Jack. But Jack is a con artist. He apologized, admitted he was a snake, and Marcie forgave him.

We all tried to talk her out of marrying Jack. Told her she was signing up for a life of deceit and misery. She'd always be watching over her shoulder, I warned.

Even the morning of the wedding, Candy and my mother spent hours with Marcie in the hotel wedding suite bathroom with a bag of ice, cucumber slices and hot towels, trying to reduce the swelling in Marcie's eyes. From crying. But Marcie had to have Jack, and now she's got him!

But does she, I wonder?

14 Spies R Us

In the morning, I whip up a quick banana bread and brew coffee, tidying up the front porch while everyone sleeps. My eyes slide to the side, secretly watching the Australian woman across the way. Her children swing on the hammock, hitting each other with Pillow Pets. Her long hair touselled, she sits staring forward, long legs pulled up to her chest. Fully clothed, thank goodness, in a long white eyelet prairie skirt and a black t-shirt. Her face reminds me of a goldfish, lips pursing and releasing, pursing and releasing, as though Earth's atmosphere hasn't enough air. Her left hand surprisingly bare, although she's the type who should be a regular at Harry Winston's. *Single? Not for long.*

Quietly, her mother passes in and out through the screen door, carrying trays and napkins and what have you. Her mother must be about 60 but she looks 50. More blonde than gray, her hair in a chignon. Her loose black pants and white tank top, Eileen Fisher. The kids finally settle down behind cereal bowls.

Day before yesterday, I noticed their white Range Rover parked on Glades Road behind their cottage. As I sweep the porch floor, I start to wonder, why did they choose Miner's Beach? A woman like that, a family like that—should be on Nantucket! Or The Vineyard. Or The Hamptons. Not Wintusket!

But hey. At least she's wearing a skirt and a shirt. Upon second thought, I suspect—*not for long.*

15 A Line In The Sand

Candy already filled me in about The Old Lady. So guess who confronts me behind the house, as I carry a trash bag of lobster and clam shells to the dumpster?

"Don't you put those stinking shells in my dumpster!" she screams at me. "We'll have horse flies from here to high heaven!"

She thinks I'll apologize. She's wrong.

"Don't worry lady. All the horse flies are in my rental house. Maybe this will draw them out!" My sarcasm is lost on her. I pry open the dumpster lid.

"Don't you dare!" She raises her stick at me.

Can you believe this? First of all, I am taking garbage out. Me! Because there's no garbage disposal or trash compacter in that rat trap of a rental house. Secondly, I'm being *yelled at by my crazy landlord. Can you imagine? I mean, me?*

I turn to her, a hand on my hip. "Okay. Where am I supposed to put them?"

She's trembling and pointing her cane in my face, reeking of BO. "You can shove them up your keister!" the Old Lady instructs, then she turns on her cane and starts to shuffle away from me. But she ain't getting away with talking to me *like that! Oh no she ain't!*

I drop the bag on the ground, open it, and pull out a lobster carcass. I start to unbutton my shorts. She turns. I pull down my shorts. They drop to my ankles. I pretend to bring the lobster shell to my crotch.

"Stop that! Stop that you!" She stomps right up to me and gets in my face, waving that stick. I hold the lobster carcass below my ass and innocently reply, "Oh I was just going to shove these up my keister, like you said!"

She's speechless.

I smile and throw the lobster in the dumpster, her hand flailing—"I said don't put that in there!—"

I pull up my shorts and button them. "Listen you basket case! I am paying you three thousand dollars a week to stay in that shit hole you call a beach house without a freaking air conditioner!"

She recedes with a crafty turn of her head. "You should have checked your lease."

"The mattresses date back to Pearl Harbor!"

"Talk to the realtor."

"Oh you betcha I will. And I'm gonna tag your listing on Craigs List!"

She blinks, pretends she knows what I mean, but I've set her little chipmunk brain in motion, *ha ha!*

I throw the bag in the dumpster and slam it shut. Heading back, I'm greeted by Candy's guargantuan ass at the head of the stairs. She doesn't realize I'm standing right behind her.

"Excuse me! Hey Candy! I'm right behind you!" I wave my hand, thinking Jack is sort of right about her being a whale. "Oh sorry!"

She turns and steps aside. Squeezing by, I see that Candy's spying on that Australian woman across the way. "Shhhhhh!" She warns.

"Get a load of this," I hiss, stomp cross the porch, slam through the screen door into the incinerator kitchen. I sit at the table, Candy anxiously behind me. "What? What?"

"You're not going to believe this! I was just reprimanded by that Beach Cottage Nazi for trying to throw a bag of shells in the dumpster!"

Candy slathers a slice of bread with Philadelphia Cream Cheese.

"Oh, her bark is worse than her bite," Candy shrugs and takes a bite.

"I'm paying *how much* to be here? To sleep with fleas and be spoken to like I'm her hired help?"

Candy gives me her calm "I-know-you-better-than-you know-yourself" voice. "Oh Marcie, will you please relax? It's just five more days!"

"Candy! I'd love to relax! Every time I try, suddenly there she is, yelling! Five more days of her popping-up out of nowhere? *This is my land!*" Candy laughs at my imitation.

"Just let it go, Marce."

"Last night, I killed over sixty mosquitoes. This morning in the shower, it was a Mexican stand-off between me and a tick the size of a Tic Tac! The tap water is yellow! We have a black and white TV! And I'm getting verbally abused for bringing a kayak and putting garbage in the dumpster? Am I paying to be punished?"

"Marcie, you just have to let it go. Have a slice."

I wince, "Geez Candy, this SUCKS!"

Candy shrugs and chews.

"I am going to talk to that realtor. Now."

"Want me to watch the kids?" she asks, her mouth full.

"Oh you're coming with me, missy." I know I sound like a total bitch, *but bitch I'll be* until things are right.

"Okay. I'll get my purse!"

"I'll be outside," I hiss, slamming the door.

16 Talking Turkey

Upstairs, I collect my bag and sunglasses from the bureau. Richard and the kids are all sleeping in the master bed, although I can't really call it a master. It has no bathrooms or closets. The kids' faces are glazed, their arms and legs covered with mosquito bites. As I smooth on some lip gloss and run a brush through my hair, I remind myself, this is the way families used to vacation on the beach. And while I love the idea of an old "camp" style beach house, not everyone else does. I should have done a better job describing these houses to Marcie.

Descending the stairs, they bend beneath my weight. *I have to go on a diet, I remind myself.* I admit it—I have been ducking the calls from my Jenny Craig advisor. Noticing the worn, sandy floorboards, the dust-drenched maritime-themed knick knacks, the filthy curtains and grimy couch, I think, maybe Marcie's right.

17 *Kiddie Time*

Madison shifts her weight, teetering on the rock, her toes wiggling for a safe indentation.

"Stay perfectly still," Jack Junior commands. *"Stay still I said!* The crabs can see your shadow, so don't move!"

Madison stays still.

"Now . . . slowly put your hand in the water." Jack Jr. sure likes giving instructions. The crab is poised, still, inches beneath Madison's hand.

Madison hesitates. "But what if it bites me?"

"Do it *you wuss!*" he yells. Jack Junior's hands are on his knees as he supervises from a square rock in the middle of the tide pool. He wears his swim trunks pulled low so you can see the elastic band of his Ralph Lauren boxers. His eyes zoom back and forth, his mouth slightly open, eager, excited—Jack Junior has a face that shouts to the world, *life is awesome!*

Not like suspicious old Madison. She looks like she's a German spy. Geez I wish she'd lighten up. She puts her hand in the water, gets scared, pulls back. She stumbles a little but rights herself.

"Chicken!" Jack yells, victorious. He does a little dance.

"They'll bite me!" she accuses.

"Bite me!" Jack Junior laughs in her face.

Enter the twins, Hailey and Bailey, in matching pink swimsuits, reassuring Madison, "They're tiny little hermit crabs! Their claws are little bitty ones!" The twins' coltish legs surf the rocks without a misstep. Their attempt to reassure Madison only makes her feel like a baby. A plump, scared little baby.

"I can't do it!" Madison shouts. Luckily, super hero older brother Austin, me, comes to her rescue. "Here's one! Have this one!"

I hand her a struggling hermit crab. She recoils.

"No!"

"He's all yours." I toss it into her bucket. Madison smiles. She's happy to have a hermit crab in her bucket at last. All the kids on the beach fill their buckets with crustaceans and compare. It's like a contest.

Madison inches her way down, finally hitting sand, she runs, kind of like a whacky walker, up to our towel. Dad sits there reading a paper. I don't know where Mom went.

The tide is going out fast. Jack Jr. and I catch like a million hermit crabs. I fill up my bucket. I use my hands, no net. We work our way around Diver's Rock. As the tide retreats, the back of the rock is revealed, covered with cascades of greenish brown sea weed. They feel like strips of rubber with rounded tips. The crabs hide underneath at the water line. I'm running my hands through sweeps of seaweed, and something bites my hand. It doesn't hurt. But I go after the creature, and awesome! "It's a lobster!" I yell.

Not a little one. A medium-sized one. Of course, it looks like an effing monster to me. I go after it, grab it around the middle and pull it out. Jack is watching me. The lobster is speckled brown and his claws are snapping angrily. I stretch my arm for my bucket. I can't reach it, so Jack grabs it, wades his way over to me and holds out my bucket. I go to drop the lobster in, and Jack pulls the bucket away so the effing lobster falls back in the water.

"You sonofabitch."

Jack says, "Oh so you're saying, your father's sister is a bitch, that's what you're saying bitch?"

"I ain't nobody's bitch."

"You go fuck yourself."

"My dick is long enough to do that."

"Yeah right."

Then I take off after the lobster. Jack's close behind, thinking he can beat me running, but I'm diving in the water. I can open my eyes underwater, so I see the lobster booking it across the sand. And then, I see Jack's legs running past me, in the water, and he reaches down and grabs the lobster. My lobster.

So I go after him, I'm going to kick his guts out. We're running, splashing through the water, I've got my arm around his neck, he's got the lobster in his right hand, and suddenly, there's Uncle Jack yelling, "Austin! Austin! Stop it!"

So I let go of Jack Jr., and of course he parades around like he's the winner of a monster truck rally, punching my lobster up in the air. Uncle Jack is yelling at us, but he's looking at me. "You gotta cut it out you two."

"Look Dad, I caught a lobster!" Jack Junior lies to his Dad.

"It's mine!"

Jack Junior attempts to cover my mouth.

"I caught the lobster Uncle Jack. Jack Junior stole it from me."

"Both of you cut it out. Somebody's gonna get hurt."

So I feel like nothing, once again.

Walking behind Uncle Jack and Jack Junior, they really are the same. They both walk like roosters, their hair blowing in the breeze. And girls are looking at them. Girls don't look at me.

Mom won't let me have long hair. I have a buzz cut, because it's sensible. I hate sensible.

We go up to the towels. The naked lady isn't there. She's sitting up on her porch with her clothes on. I wish she'd come back out, wearing a bikini, but one that covers her. Nobody would get mad at her if she just wore a normal bikini.

I'm hungry, but Mom and Aunt Marcie aren't there. Dad and Uncle Jack are reading. Jack Junior and the twins are back on the crab trail. Madison is just laying on a towel with her head down. She hates being here. She'd rather be back at home, reading her stupid Babysitting books and watching Mom cook.

I don't want to be home. I like being here. I just want to be someone else. I want to be the guy girls look at. Now I see Jack Junior on the top of Miner's Rock, jumping around. So I decide to go up there. I like going up Miner's Rock. Choosing the exact right places to put my feet and hands as I go up. Mom showed me just how to climb up Miner's Rock, the secrets of how to get up there really fast.

I saw that old brown picture of the stairs that used to be on Miner's Rock. As I crawl up, I can see the rusty holes they'd drilled centuries ago, to bolt the stairs to the side of the rock. Wish the stairs were still there.

Being on top of Miner's Rock is like visiting another planet. First, I'm up high, above everyone, like an astronaut exploring. The top of the rock is all golden with a surface of little yellowy orange pixels.

Jack Junior is jumping along the dark strip that runs over the top—the part that Mom told me not to go on. Jack Junior knows—from his mother—not to walk on the dark strip but he doesn't care—he's *jumping* on it! Jack Junior is the kind of kid who runs with scissors, falls and tells his Mom that some kid tripped him.

I explore in the opposite direction, to the right, where there's like this nature-made patio. Seriously. This shelf of a patio that overlooks Elephant Rock. Sitting there, you can watch all the teenagers diving off the back of Elephant, sliding down it's smooth nose bridge. Right now, it's low tide so nobody's on Elephant. Everyone's catching crabs over by Diver's Rock.

I love this rock patio. It's cool. I can see the curve of the land, the long stretch of the coastline, dotted with houses that disappear to the end. But then I remember I should be doing stuff, burning calories, so I get up. And I go up to the top of the rock and see Jack over toward the back of Miner's Rock. He's bent over, staring down at something. So I go over.

Jack is looking down into a hole. A big dark hole.

"This is why they call it Miner's Rock!" Jack tells me. "See? It's a tunnel. Like a mine. Like, listen to me Austin," he believes he's some kind of a teacher, "this is a mine that runs all the way down the bottom and out the rear end of the rock."

"Let's take a look."

We run down the front of the rock onto the sand, take a hairpin turn to the left, around Elephant Rock, hopping over many barnacle-covered rocks, and we pull up close to the rear of Miner's Rock. It's like the pooping end of Miner's Rock. I look up and see all the twists and turns in the mine, all different colors of rock. I'm like a geologist, studying the ancient ruins of some crazy place.

"Let's go back to the top," Jack commands.

We race up. Of course he beats me. We go up to the opening of the well. The tide is at its lowest. We both stare down the hole. Jack says, "Let's go down it!" He stares at me, his will drilling into my eyes. "I dare ya!"

We both turn at the same time to look back at the towel. Madison is asleep. Uncle Jack and the twins are gone, probably in their house for the twin's nap. My Dad is sitting on the front porch of our cottage. The Australian lady is laying in the hammock on her porch. The Crazy Old Lady sits in a plastic beach chair, just waiting for some infraction, wielding her stick. The Moms are nowhere to be seen.

Jack lowers himself into the hole. Jack's so thin his shoulder blades look like wings as he snakes his way down, he bends and shimmies, contorts and slivers down the hole. I follow. I do pretty well until I'm faced with a bulbous rock and another really pointy rock scraping my back. Despite the pain, I place my feet on lower ledges, and snake my way down. It gets darker. I look below my feet. Nothing but darkness.

"Can't chicken out now, Austin!"

"I'm not chickening out you cunt."

This is when it begins to get tight, my belly gets caught on a round of rock sticking out, and my rear end is wedged against a wall of really rough rock. My back stings, so I stay put. Jack yells, "What are you doing, you pussy?"

"Don't get your panties in a twist, Nancy!" I yell down.

Looking around, I'm mid-tunnel. Up, the sun pours into my eyes. Below, there's nothing but darkness and the incoming water. Jack Junior is gone.

So I start to shimmy down, but that makes it worse. My stomach is like *stabbed* by this rock. My back is tight against the rock behind me. A rake of barnacles feels like nails digging into my skin. Sweat pours down my back into the water. I take my feet off of their holds, and find I can just hang there. That's when I know for sure: I'm stuck. I'm stuck in the tunnel of Miner's Rock with the tide coming in.

Observation: Business etiquette for women, 1957

All ladies shall arrive at the office in hats and white gloves.

Pants or culottes are not allowed.

Ladies must type at least 60 wpm.

Coffee making skills mandatory.

Pleasant phone manner required.

Half-hour lunch break from 11:30-noon, daily.

18 *Ugly Betty*

Wintusket Realty is a quaint little white cape on Main Street surrounded by blue hydrangeas, flower boxes bursting with red geraniums. The welcoming red door is open.

"Hello?" I ask aloud as I open the screen door.

"Come in!" invites a twenty year old girl, seated at a tiny front desk, sucking on a Mary Lou's iced coffee. A fan blows her pony tail

"May I help you?" She doesn't appear to want to help.

"Ah yes, we're here to see Betty Ross."

"Just one moment," slowly, the girl emerges from behind the desk, wearing flip flops, tiny denim shorts, a tank top over a clearly visible bra. She has a tattoo of a dragon on her shoulder.

Candy and I exchange that look of dread—*oh dear God help us when our girls are teenagers.* "Shoot me please if Hailey or Bailey get tattoos, okay?" I whisper.

"And vice versa," Candy whispers back.

The charm-filled lobby is festooned with fishing nets, over sized scallop shells and dried starfish, toile wallpaper and fluffy ruffled curtains. We settle in the white wicker chairs and blue cushions. I open *South Shore Living* magazine, Candy grabs *Good Housekeeping* and unwraps a strawberry hard candy. As I page through the magazine, I understand that this area is on a lifestyle par with Princeton, New Jersey.

Little framed photographs of available homes captioned with real estate info cover the walls. "Look how reasonable these prices are!" I wonder aloud.

"May I show you something?" Betty Ross stands in the lobby, extending a hand. Her profile, unapologetically mannish and suitable for the side of Mount Rushmore, takes me by surprise. *Is that a wig she's wearing?*

"Oh, I was just noting these prices are so much lower than Jersey shore houses," I smile as Candy giggles girlishly.

"I'll be happy to show you a bargain!" Betty crows. She's tall, wearing a crisp shirtdress and an elaborate red silk scarf around her neck. She wears stockings and blue heels. Her glasses are thick, with little diamonds at the points. She wears many bracelets and rings, but not in a tacky way. Seventy years old at least, but steady on her feet, her back and neck are rim rod straight. She is not attractive, but she is imposing. All business.

"Hi, I'm Marcie White," I shake Betty's hand.

"I'm Candy Grant," Candy shakes Betty's hand, her upper arm fat wagging.

"We're the tenants at Red Rock and Beach Rock cottages. My mouth is a line, preparing to deliver a litany of complaints.

"Yes, please, this way." We follow her into a neatly organized office. "May I bring you a beverage? A gin and tonic? I have a very nice savingnon blanc on ice?" Candy and I just look at each other. It's eleven o'clock in the morning.

She claps her hands.

"I know!" She shouts. "Bloody Marys! Tiffany! Three Bloody Marys darling."

"Yes Mrs. Ross," Tiffany, of the shorts, flip flops and dragon tattoo, replies and bumps off to the kitchen.

"So! Ladies. You've come quite a long way to vacation in our beautiful seaside town!" Her dentures beam, her eyes are unblinking.

"Uh well, yes. I drove from Princeton, and Candy here drove up from Short Hills."

Candy chimes in, "We usually vacation together on the Jersey Shore."

"We're sister-in-laws."

"But this year I convinced everybody to come here, to Wintusket!" Candy's necks jiggle.

"Oh, you grew up here?"

"No we summered here."

"Where did you stay?"

"We rented on Briggs Road. The house next to the Flaherty's"

"Really? Which side of the Flaherty's?"

"To the right."

"Oh that's a grand place!" Candy has gained new respect in Betty's eyes.

"Yes, but one year we stayed at Beach Rock Cottage, and I always loved it, so when I saw on the internet it was still available, I jumped at the chance—"

"Rather impetuously," I add.

Just then, our drinks arrive, garnished with celery stalks, olives, and swimming with horseradish, placed on lovely seashell coasters. "Wow!" I exclaim.

Candy takes a sip, "This is the Martha Stewart mix, isn't it?"

Betty crows once again, "My goodness, I'm impressed!"

Candy and Betty are now in the sisterhood of Martha Stewart. "Oh I watch Martha Stewart religiously."

I take a long swallow, it is a perfect bloody mary. Tiffany reappears with a tray of mini quiches, napkins and little antique dessert plates with forks. I take a nibble of quiche. It's so cheesy with nicely done pieces of bacon. Betty eyes us as she takes another sip of her drink.

Now I realize this woman is a master manipulator. Our little brunch is not the impromptu affair it appears to be. Betty Ross has been waiting for us, knowing full well we'd arrive to get out of the lease. I decide I'd better get to the point before she gets me half shit-faced. "Uh Betty, this is so nice of you. On such short notice."

"Yes! So nice of you . . ." Candy mutters with her mouth full! Honestly, what happened to her manners?

"It's my pleasure. I'm so happy you dropped by, because I have some real bargains, what with the economy the way it is—"

I interrupt her. "Well, sorry, but we're not here to look at real estate. It's about Red Rock Cottage—"

"And Beach Rock Cottage—" chimes in Candy. "We're a little—"

"Not just a little—"

"Okay, a lot, I mean very much-"

"—shocked by the poor condition of these rentals." There. I've said it.

Betty cocks her head to the left, to the right. "Oh dear. How awful for you."

Her words don't bode well for this negotiation.

"Listen Betty. These rentals are unacceptable. They're filthy. Certainly not worth three thousand." Somebody's got to say it.

Betty is methodically pulling two files from a blue filing cabinet hand-painted with seashells. "Let's take a look at the rental agreements, ladies."

"Okay, lets," I nod, sensing we're not gaining any ground.

"Says here, in the fine print, and I hate the fine print ladies! Oh for the days when I used to rent a cottage on a handshake! Here it is. Well let me see—Rental is "as is." No smoking, no pets. No refunds." She looks up from the paper work. "Seems as though—"

I exhale loudly through my nose. "Betty, Red Rock Cottage has a mini refrigerator. I can't even fit a gallon of milk in it. There's no air conditioning. The mattresses are antiques. I hate to think what's living in them."

Betty leans forward and puts her elbows on the desk.

"Now Candy. I remember responding to your email from our Craigs List posting, correct?" Betty's sounding more like a lawyer now.

"Right . . ." Candy's half way through her bloody mary. Come to think of it, so am I.

"We spoke on the phone, and I recall asking you if you wanted to tour these rentals before signing the leases?"

"Yes, but—" Candy literally guffaws . . . "all the way from New Jersey? I couldn't leave the kids—"

Mrs. Ross turns her head to the side apologetically, "Well my dear that was your chance to examine the cottages—"

"Okay, okay you listen to me," I interrupt. My voice is flat. "The lease doesn't say anything about the harassment we're getting from this woman, Mrs. Briggs, coming over and reprimanding us all the time—!"

"Yelling at us!" Candy waves her hands in frustration.

"Mrs. Briggs is harrassing us about everything from where we put our kayak to hanging up a hose."

"Oh no."

"She wouldn't let Marcie throw clam shells in the dumpster."

"That's terrible!"

"She walked right into Candy's cottage the other night without any invitation."

"Really?"

"She wears a nightgown or bathrobe all day—she—"

"Bathrobe?"

"And she points this stick on our faces!"

"Dear me," shaking her head with false pity, Betty sighs, "Gloria is a dear old friend of mine," Betty confides, removing her glasses, "but she's terribly old and not herself. I wish you could have known her as I did, when Gloria Briggs was charming to her cottage guests. But. We all get old someday . . ." she winks at us.

"What are you going to do about it?" I must get some kind of concession. I must.

"What would you suggest I do? Sedate her? Put her in a home?"

"Couldn't she spend the week here with you?" My attempt at being funny.

Betty chuckles mirthlessly. "I suppose I could call her son—maybe he can make an effort to keep her inside."

"Yes! Please! Call the son!" I implore.

Having polished off another quiche, Candy adds, "I've never seen the son. I didn't know she had one."

I do my Crazy old lady imitation. "This is my beach!" She shouts at us all the tine, like she's God. I mean, she thinks he owns the beach!"

Mrs. Ross declares, "Well ladies, the fact is, Gloria Briggs is not crazy. The end of Brigg's Beach is her property, with the exception of Curtis House."

We freeze in disbelief.

"Everything starting from Mrs. Briggs's property line to the Curtis property line belongs to Mrs. Briggs. The rocks, the ocean, the sand, everything."

"Explain this to me, how is it not a public beach?"

"The town owns the segment of the beach to the right of the property line, where the sea wall begins. Where the lifeguards stand. That's the beginning of the town-owned portion of Miner's Rock."

"So everything to the left of that line is hers?"

"Yes."

"Oh my God! It must be worth a fortune."

"Oh my dear you have no idea." And then, I see Betty Ross's real passion. It's the Briggs Beach property! "The sad thing is, it will all go to her son when she passes," Betty remarks with a shade of intrigue.

"If it's not a pubic beach, how come she lets people use it?"

"People are permitted to sit at the end and climb the rocks at Mrs. Briggs's discretion."

"For Mrs. Briggs's amusement."

"Punishment!"

"Gives her people to yell at."

Candy and I sip our drinks dry. Now we know we're stuck in the lease, and Mrs. Ross knows it too.

Sympathetically, Mrs. Ross hands us two large coupons on thick pale pink paper. "I am very truly sorry, but let me make it up to you. Please enjoy a free spa visit at Sea Spa, down the street. Complimentary full body massage, manicure, pedicure, I believe they'll even throw in a facial."

19 Daddy Day Care

I'm feeding the kids peanut butter and jelly sandwiches on the porch. I'm looking at Richard on his porch. He's staring at the sexy Australian who is reclining in her bikini, in her hammock.

Where the hell are Marcie and Candy? The twins have already napped. They're drinking juice boxes while Jack chugs his Gatorade. They've taken a few bites of their sandwiches.

"Daddy, can we have some Skittles?"

"After you finish lunch." Marcie's gone. I'm stuck. The house is full of flies. I saw Madison go in for a nap. Austin's not around so there's no one for the kids to play with. I'm 100% miserable. All I want is air conditioning. Just to sit in air conditioning. Then I get a great idea!

"I KNOW! Hey kids, what do you say we go to the movies?"

"Really? What show, what show Dad?"

"I think Toy Story 3 is playing down the Harbor."

"Yayyyyyyyyy! Let's go! The kids race up to their rooms to put on shoes. They leave their wet bathing suits on the floors. I don't care. Just get me the fuck out of here into some air conditioning. As we exit the porch, I yell over to Richard, "Hey, I'm taking the kids to the movies in the Harbor, okay?"

Richard snaps out of his trance. "Uh okay Jack, good to know. What are you going to see?" He doesn't stand, because he's probably got a boner.

"Toy Story 3, I think. Listen man, I gotta get some air conditioning. I'm fading fast."

"Okay, I'll find out if my kids want to go. We'll meet you there."

"Sounds like a plan. Hey listen, do you know where Marcie is?"

"I think she and Candy went to talk to the realtor."

"Oh good. But if you see her, will you ask her to call my cell?"

"Will do."

20   *Hard to be Faithful*

The Australian woman is wearing a normal bikini today but still, an amazing bikini. It's black.

The body of the Australian woman is a lot like the landscape of Miner's Rock. The plateaus, the sudden points, the polished swirls and the flat smoothness of her stomach. How I long to run my hands over those ever changing surfaces. Longing is the word.

I am faithful to my wife. A lot of married guys I know, Jack included, aren't. They fool around. And they get away with it. It's just a fact. Because when you think about it, it's never been easier to fool around! With intimate encounter web sites, free porn, cell phones and texting, some guys I know are getting laid a few times a week. And their partners don't even know they're married.

Their wives will never know. Because the wives are too busy. The wives are worrying about the sixth grade graduation, or whether zithromax is better than amoxicillin, or whether to sell cupcakes or cookies or both at the bake sale, while their husbands are on Lavalife, instant messaging a horny divorcee or emailing pictures of their erect cocks via their cell phones. The married men are meeting their conquests in hotels. They're doing it in restaurant bathrooms. That's what is really going on.

I have not been doing that.

I've been doing what I'm supposed to be doing. And waiting. Hoping. Praying for sex.

I've been at the gym. I mow the lawn, rake the leaves and clean the gutters. I put up the Christmas tree, take down the Christmas tree, stock the firewood, spread the mulch, shovel the snow and clean the pool. I'm doing my job. I'm bringing home the bacon and watching my cholesterol. I'm being faithful.

I've been an idiot.

When did Candy and I stop having sex? We had sex, obviously, marginal as it was, at the beginning. Candy was thin, then. Beautiful. But even then, she was ashamed of her body. Our sex was short and she was always up and out of bed, racing into the bathroom to shower.

I told myself once we were married, we'd have time. We'd have hours and days to linger in bed. But that never happened. Something was always more important than having sex. The neighbors would hear us! The dog was barking! There was someone at the door! We'd be late for the party! The blood drive or the car wash or defrosting the refrigerator took precedence over our sex life.

We didn't even have sex to create Madison and Austin. Our children were the scientific products of invitro fertilization. It was me and my right hand, as always.

The Australian woman has made me remember sex.

The thing about sex is, it's the subtext of life. You can cover your eyes and pretend sex is not there. You can tell yourself sex doesn't matter. But as life constantly percolates and expands all around you, it's being fed by sex. I realize sex is all around me, all the time. It's all over TV, it's in songs, sex is in the heads of everyone, and I'm the only one who isn't having it.

Then I get it. It hits me. Candy has taken sex away from me. Without words, without my realizing it. I feel a profound sense of sadness. Like I'm going to cry.

Then I look up. I'm at the beach. I wonder, where is Austin? I saw Madison go in the house, but I haven't seen Austin.

21 Kid Rock

Where is Jack Jr.? He knows I'm stuck here.

I can hear kids playing on the rock above my head. Below, the water rises, sloshing around, echoing. It's still not high tide, so I think. I hurt all over. I know I'm bleeding down into the water—which is a little like a dinner invitation to the sharks.

I guess I was expecting Jack Junior to go get my Mom or Dad.

Yeah, but depending on Jack Junior is kind of like depending on Sponge Bob.

I keep trying to pull myself out, but now my fingers are bleeding. I don't want to start yelling or calling for help, because I'll feel like a fool. I imagine the newspaper headline now, "Fat boy gets stuck in Miner's Rock."

How uncool. I gotta get out of here without a fuss, or embarrassment. The slosh of the incoming water echoes through the well and it's hard to hear. I think I hear my Dad calling me. But maybe I'm imagining it. I hate to cry. It's so wimpy. But I'm crying now.

22 Bad Dad

"Austin? Austin!" I yell, walking up and down, in the surf.
I tell the lifeguards my son is missing, and they tell me, "We can look for him from this line on. But over to the left, it's a privately owned beach."

I'm kind of shocked. "What, you won't help me find my kid?"

They're young male jocks with oatmeal for brains. "We'll try. Okay mister? See what we can do."

A whistle is blown, a sense of alert overtakes the beach. A tanned, six-pack ab 18-year-old guy with long sun bleached hair announces through a bullhorn, "a boy is missing. Black swim trunks. His name is Austin. If anyone has any information, please tell us."

One of the lifeguards shoots into the water on his red cross surfboard. Another gets on a walkie talkie and alerts the fire department. I hear a siren in the distance. I begin to feel better, that something is being done. I turn, and there is Madison, her face hot and flushed from her nap. "Dad, what's going on?"

"Oh honey," I kneel before her. Her giant blue eyes stare at mine. "Austin is missing."

"Oh Daddy!" she begins to cry. "Where's Mommy?"

All of a sudden, who arrives in her pajamas and cane but Gloria Briggs. "What's wrong?"

The last thing I want is to pull this nutcase into the situation. "Uhh, my son? Austin? I can't find him."

She stumbles a little, seeking balance in the sand, I see my information processing through her cloudy eyes. She nods a lot and says to me, "Did you check The Mine?"

"What mine?" I wonder aloud.

"In the rock."

"Where?"

"Come, come, now! Hurry."

I'm thinking the police and fire department are a better bet. The sirens are getting closer.

Suddenly, I'm hit on the back of my neck with her cane. Mrs. Briggs is quickly hobbling through the sand toward the rock. "Hurry up! The tide's coming in!"

I look around. The lifeguards are heading east. Madison runs ahead of Mrs. Briggs crying, "Hurry Daddy!"

I follow, blindly, I run across a sandcastle and the little kids protest, "Hey Mister!"

I run to the base of the rock where Mrs. Briggs stands supported by her cane. She commands, "Get up there! Go!"

I crawl up after Madison, both of us struggling.

"Get up there! Now go to the middle!" I race up there, my head reeling, trying to find the spot Mrs. Briggs is yelling about. Madison finds it first. "DADDY! Here!"

She's kneeling in front of a hole in the rock, crying, reaching down, "Austin! It's okay! Daddy's here!"

Right behind her, I stare into the hole, and I see the top of Austin's head and hear him crying, "Daddy, daddy! I'm stuck! I can't get out!"

Flat on my stomach, I stretch my arms down, but I can't touch him. "Madison! Go tell the lifeguards that Austin's stuck here!"

She's crying so hard. "Daddy!"

"Please Madison, go!" I can hear the tide coming. The waves are licking the back of Elephant Rock. "Okay Daddy!" She stumbles off.

"Austin! Austin! Talk to me!"

Austin emits this long, low bay, like a trapped animal. "Daaaaaaaad. Daaaaaaad." He's crying.

Still down on my stomach, I crawl face first into the hole, "It's gonna be all right."

"Daaaaaaaaaaaad!"

"Buddy! Buddy! We'll get you out of here!"

"You can't." He moans.

"Believe me." Encouragement.

"I'm stuck." Despair.

"Trust me." I can almost reach his hand.

"I want Mom." Fear.

"Can you raise you arm up?"

"Ahhhhhhhhhh!" I hear him freaking out, "Dad the water is touching my feet now."

"How long have you been here?"

"Da-aaa-ddd-yyyy. I don't know. A-a-ah-while . . . ."

"Try to reach my hand."

"Ohhhhh kay."

I hold his hand. It's cold. So cold. "Oh Dad. Oh Dad. Thank you Dad." The contact has calmed him. But I'm holding myself above the hole with my legs. That's all that's holding me. Suddenly, three lifeguards are there with a chain fire ladder and a rope.

"Don't move sir."

"I'm holding his hand."

Hearing strange voices, Austin shrieks, "Daddy!"

"It's okay Austin, we've got some professional help."

By then the sirens fill our ears. Uniformed fire and police carry equipment across the beach. I hear their walkie talkies and the unleashing of their ladders and hooks. "Daaaaady—I'm so—(hiccup hiccup)—sorry."

"It's okay, hold on Austin, just hold on."

Austin squeezes my fingers as hard as he can, but I know he's lost a lot of heat. He's crying, nervous over the rising tide.

"Daaaaa-dy . . . Daaaaaaa-dy." I try to go deeper in, but someone grabs my ankles and in a gruff voice order, "Sir, you're going to have to let go."

Now I'm crying, "Not on your life."

Alarmed, Austin's cry is worse. "Daaaaaad. Don't let go."

A firefighter shouts down to Austin, "Son, your Dad has to let go so I can get you. I'm Captain Gary Mahoney. I will get you son. I've been trained to do this, I've gotten kids out of this hole before, so you just have to trust me. Let go sir. Please."

Austin is sobbing, terrified, "Ohhh—kaaaaay. Daddy, Dad."

The firefighters pull me out of there like I'm a rag doll, and another firefighter walks me down the rock, holding me tight, which I appreciate because I'm shaking uncontrollably. "He's gonna be okay. We rescue one of these kids from that hole every summer."

"Thank you." My voice is trembling. He gets me to the sand, and Madison is on me like glue. She's crying, I'm trying not to cry, as we watch the emergency rescue workers on the rock, trying to extricate Austin. Crowds of beachgoers have gathered, their arms folded, watching. I yearn to be them, just a bystander. My son is the one trapped in there.

Madison says what's on my mind in a gravely voice, "Where is Mommy?"

23 Psychic Powers

I don't know who I am, where I am . . . I am drifting on a cloud . . . I am nothing but a wisp floating . . . a lily pad . . . a fairy . . . a bird. I am a flower, so deep in, so relaxed.

The masseuse whispers, "Hello Candy! Now it's time to turn over on your back . . ."

It takes a bit of doing, but I turn over, sorry that the masseuse will no longer be working the knots in my shoulders. My eyes open a crack, and I see Marcie on the other table alongside me, in a similar state of optimum being.

I've never had a full body massage before. I always felt too ashamed to be naked in front of a stranger. But this, this, this feeling is so amazing! I will be having more of these, more and more.

What a state of relaxation! Marcie and I have our nails and toes done. Facials that seemed to awaken every pore of my face. And now, now *this*. So, erotic in a way. I've never had such an all over experience. Not even sex with Richard is this good! Even the tips of my toes and the ends of my fingers have been totally and utterly caressed. I've never been more relaxed.

The massage therapist whispers, "Now Candy, I am going to leave the room. You can rest for a moment, reawaken your senses, and then get dressed. I'll see you in the lobby."

My mind goes from black to the pale filterings of present day, *"This is over?"*

Marcie sighs and moans, "How 'bout another half hour. I'll pay."

Suddenly, I hear a splitting ambulance siren. Usually, sirens pass over me as somebody else's business. But this time is different. A stark claw grips my heart. I sit bolt upright on the table and sense a real feeling of panic. A voice, a presence, a feeling overwhelms me. *I know it's my kid.* Not sure if it's Austin or Madison. *But it's my kid. I just know it's my kid.*

"Marcie, let's get out of here." My feet are on the floor, I'm pulling my clothes on.

"Candy, chill, will ya?" Marcie's half asleep.

I'm desperate. "Call me crazy but something's wrong. Very very very wrong Marcie. Those sirens are for me. I just know it! It's Austin or Madison."

"Cut it out." Marcie mumbles. "I'm staying. Take my keys. I'll catch a cab back."

"Okay I'm taking your keys," I call behind me, as I sail through the lobby. I shout to the receptionist, "I'll leave a tip later, I gotta go."

24 Like Father, Like Son

Woody, Buzz and their entourage are finally safe and it looks like the world of toys will go on. As we exit the movie theater, the twins are eating gummy worms and Jack Junior is eyeing the t-shirts for sale. I'm reluctant to leave this world of air conditioning, sand-free carpeting and toilets that flush. As we head for the door, Jack Junior looks up at me, saying "Can I tell you something Dad?"

"Yes?" I'm putting on my shades and reaching for my keys, checking for messages on my cell. Gwen has left five voicemails.

I open the theater door for the kids. We're hit by a wall of heat and humidity. I groan. As we walk toward my Porsche, Jack pipes up, "Dad, I think I should tell you something."

"What?"

"Well, you should have checked with Austin to see if he wanted to come to the movies."

"Yeah, but he was taking a nap."

"Uh, Dad, no he wasn't. That's why you should have checked harder."

"What do you mean . . . Should have checked *harder?*"

"Yeah see Dad, Austin couldn't come, 'cuz he's stuck in this big old hole in the middle of the big rock."

I stop, holding the twin's hands. "What?"

Jack Jr. appears uncomfortable, twisting his fingers. "Dad, I forgot. Austin is stuck in the big rock. In a hole."

"You left him there?"

"I forgot!"

"Who else knows about this?"

"Nobody?"

There are many reasons why I have a 911 GT 2, and this is best one yet. "Hold on kids," I shout as I tear down Main Street to Miner's Beach.

Jack is crying, "Dad, Austin's so fat, he got stuck. I made it down just fine! It's 'cuz Austin is *so fat*, that's why! Dad? You're not mad at me Dad?"

As we ease into the phalanx of fire trucks, police cruisers and ambulances, I'm told again and again that we're not permitted entry. All the kids are crying. As one police officer after another questions us, I explain we're renting Red Rock Cottage and my nephew is the one who's in trouble. "Is he alive," I ask.

"Yes sir, he made it."

Jack looks up at me, vindicated, sighing, "See Dad? I told you."

25 On The Road

Apparently, there is no taxi service in Wintusket, Massachusetts. So all the spa receptionist could do was give me a map of Wintusket, a bottle of water and some body lotion samples before I set off on foot to get back to the rental cottage.

My shoe choice: quite unfortunate. My brand new low-heeled leather flip flops were not meant for long walks. The sharp strips cut into my toes, road dust powders my feet and legs. But I walk on. No cars on the road. Everybody's at the beach. Of course I try calling Jack, Richard and Candy repeatedly, but no one picks up. They don't have service.

My fury fuels every step over the two miles I walk. Between my toes I'm bleeding. I've removed the flip flops and my bare feet burn on the molten heat of the road.

As I limp onto Miner's Beach Road, I see flashing lights and police cars and a lot of emergency vehicles thrumming down the end, outside of our rental houses. I pick up my pace. Maybe Candy was right. I start running.

26 To The Rescue

Firefighters above me, passing down a ladder, coming down, and bracing me for the worst. "Okay Austin, we're going to give one big pull, and we'll pull you out, but it's gonna hurt. After that, we'll wrap you up. Then you'll be in an ambulance with your Mom on the way to the hospital."

"Mom?" I start screaming. "Mom!"

The reassuring voice returns, "Your Mom's on the beach. So you ready Austin?"

"Okay." I'm shaking. My back zizzles with pain, throbbing against the barnacles. I know my blood is dripping to the sharks. And the sharks will bite off my feet. I am going to be one of those guys in wheel chairs and I'll never play football.

Above, my arms are yanked up and the rope wrap tightens under my arms and I'm pulled upwards, a bunch of urgent voices shouting, *"Go! Go! Go!"*

My skins screams with pain. And then, I'm out. I'm being carried by a couple of really burley guys. Everybody's cheering. Everything is very blurry and gray with sudden splotches of light and faces in my face.

"Austin! God thank you! It's Mommy! I'm here!" I see Mom's face above as everything goes horizontal, I'm wrapped in a blanket, someone puts a shot in my arm and things get fuzzy, I see Dad and Madison's crying, then that weird old lady scolds and points at me, "I told you! Stay out of the mine!"

I'm about to pass out, but before I do, I tell that crazy old bat, *"No you didn't!"*

27 The Blame Shame Game

I peek through the porch window, and Jack Junior's head is on the kitchen table. I pick him up, carry him to his bed, and gently lay him down. I put a pillow under his head. He's sound asleep, which is the best way for him to be.

Marcie and the girls are all jammed in the full-sized bed, the twins sleep, one against each side of their mother's neck, they shift fitfully, tossing and murmuring. In the middle, Madison is glued to Marcie's side, her arms around her Aunt's legs, the fan blowing their hair. Madison spent the better part of the evening crying in Marcie's arms and glaring at Jack Junior.

Marcie's feet are bound in bandages. Turns out, she walked a couple miles along the side of the road in her stupid designer fashion sandals. Once she arrived on the scene and the police understood she was part of the family, they pulled her into the back of a fire truck and bandaged up her feet. They gave her Percocet.

After this hellish night, it's good to have everyone asleep so I can think. I go out on the porch. Light a cigar, discover all the ice in the cooler has melted, and pour a full glass of Jack. I've only been sipping 'til now, just waiting for everyone to shut down.

Apparently, my son has no sense of conscience, no sense of responsibility. It's my fault. I guess. I have no sense of loyalty, so why should he?

But then again, he's seven.

I recall, when I was that age, being so angry at my mother over some stupid thing that I can't even remember, I hid her car keys in a secret box by my bed. And I promptly forgot all about it. Next day, I arrived home after a sleepover at a friend's and come to find out, my mother and my sister had to take a cab to my sister's dental appointment. I thought my mother was going to kill me. I didn't watch TV for two weeks and they locked up my bicycle for the rest of the summer.

We never punish Jack Jr. like that. So he never learns consequences. *What the hell difference is a time out really gonna make?*

I look at my cell phone. Reception improved, I see Gwen's left twelve messages. *I told her not to call.* I just erase all of her messages. One thing at a time.

I think about that poor bastard Austin, stuck in that rock.

Candy's fault, feeding Austin all that crap.

Jack Junior's fault too, for not telling anyone.

My fault for not insisting to bring the cousins to the movies.

Richard's fault for not watching his kids.

The goddamn town's fault for not covering the hole.

Shame on that realtor for not warning us.

Shame on all of us.

One hundred percent. Out of curiosity, I decide to take a look at the hole. With my drink and cigar in hand, I cross the cool sand and climb up the rock. It just takes a few steps to get to the top. There's no wind. The moon blasts down on the rock's sparkling mica surface. I don't get too close to the hole. But looking down, I see the confined space below, I hear the churning of the water beneath and I shake my head. "Austin's a lucky bastard."

28 Relief and Disappointment

I wake up Thursday morning, as a nurse smoothly pushes a wheeled cart bearing a covered dish to Austin's bed. I wipe my eyes a few times, stir my tongue around in my mouth and sit up straight. The nurse murmurs, "Good morning! And how's our little survivor doing?"

Austin's eyelids flutter. Richard continues to snore.

"Here." The nurse looks at me sympathetically, handing me a cup of black coffee. I wish it had some cream and sugar. She busily checks Austin's vitals and readings on the machines.

I sip it any way. "Thank you so much."

"Let me know if you need anything."

I run a hand through my greasy hair, "I need to know what's going to happen next."

The nurse shoots me a cautionary smile. "I'm not a fortune teller." After reading my shocked expression, she turns, "The doctors will be in soon, hon."

Hon? I'm glad she's gone. My phone buzzes. "Hello?"

"It's me. Candy, I apologize for Jack Junior."

"Marcie, later."

"Okay, but—but—okay." She's crying. "But Jack Junior should have told us."

"Marcie, my son's alive. That's all I care about." I make sure to ask, "How're you?"

"Miserable. Me feet are shredded."

"I'm sorry I took the car, but I just knew one of my kids was in trouble."

"You're psychic."

"I am. How's my Madison?"

"Sullen. Angry. Feeling abandoned."

"Oh dear. I'm sorry." You'd think, just this once, Marcie could just say something like, "Madison's fine" but no.

Suddenly the doors burst open, the curtain is jerked open, a dozen doctors in various garb surround Austin's bed, some consult tablet computers, others fiddle with monitors.

"Gotta go. I'll call you back later."

They tell me they've seen this one before. Guess a couple of kids have ended up here after being stuck in the same hole. Again, I'm shocked. No one warned us. No one person.

They roll Austin into a special exam room. They ask me to leave, but I won't, so I have to surgically scrub-in at a sink and change into scrubs. I pull on a mask and gloves. How ca*n Richard sleep through this?*

All the doctors back off when they unwrap Austin. He's still knocked out. From my vantage point, I get a full view, and tears immediately leap into my eyes. Austin's skin is really torn up. His front side has comparatively marginal wounds, but they're deep. His fingertips are torn. Remarkably, his face is fine.

I'm worried, now that they've unwrapped him, they're exposing him to God knows what infection. I can't hear what they're saying. I'm scared. I turn and find Richard standing on the other side of the glass, he's mouthing "what's going on?" to me. His eyes look like bullet wounds. I know he's had a rough time but Jesus, he can't even watch our children while I'm gone?

A doctor emerges, her hands held high, tinged with blood. "We want to move him to Children's Hospital."

I say yes and Richard mouths "What?" through the glass as I sign a release form.

We follow the ambulance into Boston. I'm at the wheel, Richard is too shaky to drive. *You'd think, just this once, he'd take charge.*

The ambulance shoots ahead of us at the hospital, while I turn the van into a parking lot. When we walk in the doors of Children's Hospital, they extend papers for us to sign. Richard tries to sign, but the pen slips from his shaking hand. I grab a pen from my purse and sign it.

Soon, we're ushered up into a treatment room. We look through the glass as they attend to Austin's wounds.

They work precisely, with tiny forceps, delicately removing pieces of sheared skin, sand and barnacle fragments. They toss the pieces into a steel dish. They remove pieces of seaweed and tiny pebbles, they tenderly gauze away particles of sand. There isn't a lot of bleeding. Each wound is individually medicated, cleansed and covered. When they're done, they wrap Austin up and roll him into his room. He's hooked up to IVs.

Right before Richard and I fall asleep in the collapsible bedside chairs, Richard remembers something. "I forgot to tell you!"

The Boston skyline lights the side of Richard's face as he recollects with excitement.

"What?" I turn.

"You know who *really* saved Austin's life?"

"I thought it was Madison and you!"

"We never would have looked there if it weren't for the Crazy Old Lady."

I shake my head, "Oh come on?"

"*She did!* I was running in the opposite direction, thinking Austin was in the water—I was following the lifeguards! All of a sudden, the Crazy Old Lady stops me—told Madison and me to climb up Miner's Rock and check the mine hole. *That's* how Madison got to Austin. It was her. The Crazy Lady!"

"Well. What do you know."

I mask my disappointment from Richard, as I always do.

29 Escape from Wintusket

Maybe if I stay in bed long enough, I'll fall back asleep and all of this will have been a dream. Correction—a nightmare.

I close my eyes tight. Flies tap the screens and buzz, outside, the waves roll in and roll out.

I just want to be back home, in my spot on my favorite couch in my TV room, watching TV and eating Goldfish. I want my bed. My pillow. My blankets. *Why are we here? Why did we come here? I hate it here! This place stinks!*

Even though Mom was an idiot to choose this place, I still want Mom. I get so scared every time I remember, Austin could have died!

If I go downstairs, I'll have to face Jack Junior, that weasel.

If I just had my own cell phone I could at least be texting with Mom to find out what's going on. I feel so alone. There's sand in the sheets, horse fly bites all over my ankles, *I hate this place!*

I'm going to get out of here.

I'm going to make them take me to Mom.

I go down stairs. I'm still in my nightgown. All of my clothes and things are in my family's rental next door.

The twins play with naked Barbies on the front porch. Don't they ever get sick of that game? As I tip toe into the kitchen, Aunt Marcie smiles, "Hello Madison. How're you feeling today, sweetie?"

This growl pours out of me. I didn't know it was there. "I want to go to the hospital."

I don't mean to sound so angry, but I am. Aunt Marcie extends a bowl of Froot Loops *which I hate,* her eyes meet with Uncle Jack's, saying *can-you-believe-this-impossible-child?*

"Listen Pumpkin, *(Pumpkin?)* we're going to sit tight until we hear more from your Mom and Dad."

"Don't call me Pumpkin," I hiss. "I want my mother." I stomp my foot. Fold my arms. Narrow my eyes.

Aunt Marcie hovers with a glass of orange juice, which I do not take. "Madison, honey! They moved your brother to Children's Hospital in Boston, so it's probably not a good idea to-"

"Take me there now!" I scream. My demand echoes. Aunt Marcie kneels before me, her hands on my shoulders. "Oh Madison honey, I know how you feel . . ."

"No YOU DON'T!!!" I wriggle away from her, pointing, "This never would have happened if it weren't for your stupid Jack Junior!"

"Madison!" Uncle Jack snaps, comes over and kneels alongside Aunt Marcie. "You know Pumpkin—"

"STOP CALLING ME PUMPKIN!"

Aunt Marcie's head swivels in reaction to Uncle Jack while Jack Junior sits at the table, his mouth curved downward, his eyes shut. I'm glad he feels bad. I hate him.

"Jack, you suck!" I yell and run, slamming the screen door as hard as I can, past the twins, down the stairs, across the sand, up the Beach Rock Cottage steps and into our living room next door. I slam the door and lock it. I let out a ragged sigh.

Moments later, Aunt Marcie starts pounding on the door, "Madison! *Let me in!*"

I hope she yells her lungs out. I go upstairs and get out of my nightgown, looking at my pointy nipples. I'm getting boobs, but Mom won't get me a training bra, even though every girl in my class wears a bra. Maybe now she'll change her mind.

I slide into my smooth pink sundress and sandals. Aunt Marcie's still pounding and yelling down there. Let her. I look in the foggy mirror above the ancient bureau. My eyes are swollen from crying. I get my brush and brush my own hair, which I never do, but this is an emergency. I go into the bathroom, find a washcloth and wipe my eyes with cold water. That feels good. I even brush my teeth without having to be reminded.

When I open the front door, Aunt Marcie is standing there, her arms crossed, grinding her back molars. "Listen to me Madison Grant, you do not talk to me or your cousin that way, do you understand me missy?!"

I stare at her. "I'm packing a bag of clothes, toothbrushes, things like that, for Mom and Dad, and then you'll drive me to Children's Hospital."

"No I'm not."

"Then I'll hitch hike." I calmly buckle my wristwatch.

"They won't let you see your brother!"

"Fine."

"Maddie, the hospital has rules, special visiting hours . . ."

"I DON'T CARE! GET ME AWAY FROM YOUR ROTTEN KID!"

She hobbles over to a chair. Her feet are still swaddled in gauze. I forgot about her feet. "You'll forgive Jack Junior some day."

"No I won't." My calm unnerves Aunt Marcie. She sits up straight and yells, "This is not Jack Junior's fault! Your brother crawled into that hole!"

"You weren't there! So you don't know!!"

"You're going to regret these words someday." I see the ripple of veins in her forehead.

"Jack Junior *led Austin* into that hole! Because Jack Junior is a *jerk*! He pulls the arms off starfish! He spits in my soda! He pees under the porch! And he left *my brother* and went to the fucking *movies*!"

"Wait 'til I tell your mother what you just said to me!" Her eyes burn. "I'm getting your Uncle." She stands uneasily and gingerly takes the stairs, "Ow! Ouch! Ouch!"

Good.

I go upstairs, find my mom's monogrammed L.L. Bean bag tote. In my parents' room, I grab them their clean but creepy underwear. I add one of my Mom's dresses, sweater, a pair of flats, her brush, her reading glasses, make up, and other things. Dad's blue golf shirt and a pair of Dockers, his Topsiders, deodorant, razor and sunglasses. Then I go downstairs to the porch, where Uncle Jack is smoking a cigar. "Come on. I'm driving you to Children's Hospital."

I can hear Aunt Marcie yelling. "You just don't listen! Didn't I tell you . . . . !"

Jack Junior wails. The twins' Barbie game has become more complex. "Don't you give me that missy!" commands the blonde Barbie as the brunette Barbie reminds her, "He's your boyfriend! You watch him!"

Uncle Jack opens the door of his cool car. I practically have to lay down it's so low to the ground and when he revs the engine, the reverberations zizzle down my tailbone. "Thanks Uncle Jack."

"No problem."

"Uncle Jack?"

"Yuh?"

"How come you wear a bracelet?"

"Because your Aunt Marcie gave it to me."

"How come?"

"Because I don't wear rings, so I wear this."

"How come you don't wear rings?"

"I dunno, rings are uncomfortable. I like this."

"It looks reptilian." He gives me a funny look.

"Really? It's by this famous jewelry designer, David Yurman."

"Never heard of him. It's cool I guess."

"I think so."

"But I'm going to make my husband wear a ring no matter what."

"Good for you."

"Even if I have to super glue it to his finger."

"Well good luck with that," Uncle Jack looks out his window.

"I've never been in this car."

"Really? How do you like it?"

"It doesn't have a backseat."

"Doesn't need one." He puts on his Yankees baseball cap, and checks his reflection in the mirror.

"Uh . . . . Uncle Jack . . . You're not going to wear that hat are you?"

He smiles, but underneath, he's losing patience. *"Why not?"*

"Because. I just don't want you to get hit."

A sick look passes over his mouth. "Uh . . . What's that supposed to mean?"

"Uncle Jack. We're in *Boston*."

He smiles, laughs, throws the Yankees cap behind him.

"Oh yeah. You're right. I forgot."

30 *Isn't It Ironic?*

Jack Junior has cried himself to sleep upstairs. The twins are deep in a fantasy world on the porch with their Barbies, a couple American Girl horses and a bucket of crabs. I've taken another Percocet.

My feet throb. The bandages are filthy.

The monotonous buzz of flies. Dishes piled in the sink. Unmade beds. Dirty laundry on the bathroom floor. The milk has spoiled. Everywhere I look around this rat trap, something is terribly wrong, and there's nothing I can do about it.

Jack is conveniently gone, as usual, leaving me to deal with the real shit. And guess what? I can't deal with anything right now. All I can do is sit here. So I pour myself a glass of warm root beer and gingerly shuffle to a seat on the porch.

I have to laugh as I listen to Bailey speaking for her American Girl Doll. "My horse is having a baby!"

Hailey whispers, "My horse is having twins."

Bailey counters with, "My horse is having triplets."

The never-ending female game of one upmanship. I'm glad they're learning it early.

The air is dry, but still no breeze. I throw my head back and close my eyes, taking a deep breath. As I exhale, I hear the all-too-familiar scrape of Crazy Lady's cry, "You! Up there! On the porch! You! Is this your raft down here?"

I open my eyes, and turn my head to peer over the railing. "Yes it is!"

She's standing at the foot of the steps pointing at Austin's yellow raft. "You have to move this!"

"No I don't."

"What did you say?"

"Stop yelling at me and come up here." The bald pink circle on the top of her head is visible from this angle. I hear the clank of her stick on the steps, her muttering, ". . . Just leaving stuff around like a bunch of drunken sailors. Slobs! *Heathens! . . .*"

She levels her look at me. Does she notice my feet? No. "Get rid of that raft."

"Mrs. Briggs, I can't walk."

She looks at my feet with surprise, like a crow picking at a carcass. "All right then, get your boy to move it."

I stare at her, purposefully languid. "Don't tell me what to do."

"Your kids are spoiled brats!"

"Look, we're just renting your house. We didn't sign up for your Outward Bound Program."

She leans back, her mouth open, "You yuppies don't teach your kids to work."

"And free child rearing advice to boot!" I clap my hands. "All right Missus Briggs! Hailey, Bailey, please go upstairs, wake up your brother and ask him to come down here."

"Okay!" The twins love to wake people up. They race for the stairs.

Mrs. Briggs, uninvited, puts her bony ass in one of her shredded wicker chairs. "How's your nephew?"

"Why do you care?"

"I don't care. I'm curious is all."

"He's at Children's Hospital." She doesn't notice the daggers in my eyes.

"Well. He'll be all right." She looks around at the naked Barbies and toys on the porch floor. "Heathens."

Just then, Jack Junior drags himself onto the porch. He's wearing a frown, his swollen eyes are slit with resentment. "What."

"Jack, can you drag that raft up to Aunt Candy's porch?"

"I can. Doesn't mean I will."

Mrs. Briggs smiles with relish at my son's insurrection.

"I'm not asking you, I'm telling you. You get down there and put that raft on Aunt Candy's porch."

He folds his arms. "And if I don't?"

"You will stay in your bedroom until the end of time."

He goes downstairs, Mrs. Briggs is jubillent. "That's how to talk to the boy."

"Is that how you talk to *your boy?*"

"What?" She wavers.

I raise my eyebrows in innocence. "I was told you have a son. But I've never see him! I understand he's a grown man. And he lives with you. In your house. Isn't that true?"

She acts like she just remembered something. "Oh right, right. I do. I do have a son. Uh, he doesn't come outside too much. He married a Mexican Obama lover and they got a mixed race child."

"Well, why don't you send *your* son to a Home Depot? Tell him to get some new Andersen windows! With screens!"

Her lower jaw trembles, she blinks a lot. "What's that? Screens? I got perfectly good screens—"

"No you *don't* Mrs. Briggs. You got *lousy* screens!"

"You saying these screens aren't up to snuff?"

"I'm saying you make at least forty thousand dollars a summer off of these two rat traps! And you and your son can't part with one dime for upkeep?"

"What did you say to me?" She blinks and trembles.

"What kind of work ethic did you teach *your* son Mrs. Briggs? 'Cuz I haven't seen him *lift a finger* since I've been here! Tell me! Does he get up off the couch to pee or does he just pee into an old Pringles can?"

"Why the nerve of you—"

"You're telling me what to do with my son? I'll tell you what to do with yours."

"My son has allergies—"

"Allergic to work! You got rotten mattresses! Floors filthy! Oh and—by the way—ever heard of COLOR television?!"

She stands, the loose flesh under her chin flapping, "Rude! Hush you rude woman—!"

Jack comes up the stairs, "I moved the raft, Mom."

"Thank you Jack. Hey Mrs. Briggs!" I yell across the sand as she beats her retreat, "at least *my* son did *something* today!"

31 Shifting Gears

It's good to be back in the saddle, cruising up the Southeast Expressway, women staring at me in the Porsche.

It's a chick magnet. Even though I'm with The Niece from Doom. I would ordinarily say "little niece" but she ain't little. A girl this young has no business being this fat. Her thighs spread like foccacia loaves across the passenger seat.

The niece is grim. But she gives off a twinge of a smile when she sees the John Hancock Tower, the milieu along Newbury Street, the students outside of Berklee School of Music. New Jersey ain't got that, as I puff on my cigar.

When we arrive at the hospital, I drop her off at the door and I find the best place to park the Porsche. I tell her to meet me in the lobby.

When I'm parked, I check my messages. Twenty messages from Gwen. I erase them all, and call her. She answers on the first ring. "Gwen, you called me like twenty million times?"

"Cut the bullshit Jack. Where are you?"

"I am at Children's Hospital in Boston."

"What a coincidence! I'm in Boston too."

Why didn't Gwen ask me why I'm at Children's Hospital?

"Are you shittin' me?"

"I caught a train to Boston. I've been waiting for you."

"Gwen?" Meanwhile, I'm thinking, *what the fuck?*

"I'm at the Four Seasons. And if you hurry, the Jacuzzi will be hot enough for us both."

"Gwen, why'd you do such a thing?"

"Because I love you Jack."

"You're not supposed to say that, remember?"

The pitch of her voice squeaks with tears. "I've been waiting days for you! And I can't wait any more!" She sniffles. Great. I can imagine the hotel bill.

"Gwen, Gwen, Gwen, please." I look up and there's the niece.

"Who are you talking to, Uncle Jack?" Her dark little eyes are quite piercing.

Gloom and doom Madison, spying on me. I click my phone off.

I blurt out, "One of my clients, you've heard of Gweneth Paltrow, haven't you?"

"No?" Madison scowls, a trait she picked up from her Mom, The Whale.

"She won the Academy Award for Best Actress."

"Gwen Paltrow?" she tests me.

"Gweneth." I correct her.

"You called her Gwen." She's suspicious.

"What is this, an inquisition?" God this kid is a goddamn pain in the ass.

"Noooooo," she defends.

"She's my client. Now Madison, stop picking your nose. I told you to meet me in the lobby, didn't I?"

"I wasn't—"

I guide Madison through the parking garage and put the parking pass in my wallet.

After we both undergo the washing, the scrubbing and the redressing by some very sexy nurses, we enter the ICU area to find Richard and Candy wearing scrubs, masks, gloves, plastic coverings over their heads and feet, as they lean over Austin's unit. They surge to hug Madison.

"Hey guys!" I smile. My smile is not met with smiles, just pained teary-eyed cheeks and arms that hug me hard for bringing Madison to the hospital. I'm not a hugger, but I go with it, given the circumstances.

I take a few more steps into the space and get the full force of Austin's situation. He's the color of pastry dough.

"So here's a gift from Madison." I extend a plume of gift shop balloons. "He's asleep," Candy whispers anxiously. Richard looks down between his knees, hands folded.

"I brought clothes and things for you guys," Madison is pleased with their delighted reaction. I just want them to get out of there so I can think.

"Rich, Candy, you go change and get something to eat. I'll stay with Austin."

The thing is, when a kid's asleep, it's like watching an angel. Especially a kid in an ICU box covered with tubes and wires, surrounded by machines, blinking and bleeping. A doctor appears. "He's stable. His numbers are solid."

The doctor looks like he's fourteen. He's got spiked up hair, freckles across the bridge of his nose. He's got a tattoo of a mermaid on his neck. *Shit I'm getting old.*

The doctor takes off. I keep looking down at Austin, thinking how close he came. I don't blame Jack Junior specifically, although he screwed up royally. Let's face it. Austin's accident was a team effort. But to lose Austin, or any of these kids, would be something I'd never get over.

To think of it is terrifying. I let a tear get away just thinking about it.

Austin wakes up for a second, but I coax him back to sleep. I'm 100 percent sorry.

After awhile, Richard, Madison and The Whale return, all washed and dressed in fresh clothes. And I'm out the door.

"Glad I could be of service, and I uh, think I'm gonna take off now."

Richard's eyes laser into mine, "Thanks Jack."

As I walk through the ICU, I see babies the size of dolls. I see a kid with skin so burnt, he might as well be a character on Cartoon Network. Comparatively speaking, Austin's the healthiest kid in the joint.

32 Shoulda, Woulda, Coulda

I didn't mean for Austin to get stuck in that hole. I thought he would make it out.

Yeah but he's so fat. But still.

I should have told someone that Austin was stuck. I shouldn't have forgot. But I just forgot! I should have remembered.

Sitting here in the waves, the other guys are on surfboards and boogie boards. They're having all the fun that is gone for me now.

Yesterday, I was free. After what happened to Austin, today I am a different.

33 Fantasy Fight

It was nice that Jack dropped off Madison at the Hospital. But the nicest part was seeing him go white after seeing Austin. He knows *I know,* what his kid did to mine.

If I were a fighting man, and I'm not, I would hit Jack with the corner of a brick—right in the teeth. That would end that insincere asshole smile of his. Jack would have to pay thousands of dollars to replace his teeth. And I'd enjoy the period of time between dental visits, seeing him unarmed, vulnerable, without his greatest weapon.

34 Why Me?

The irony of it all.

I'm the person who *least wanted to be here*, I'm the person who wanted to leave upon arrival, I've been the most vocal critic of this whole stupid plan, and here I am, the only adult, stuck, in this rat trap, watching the kids. And I can't walk.

Jack Junior and the twins are out of their minds they're so worn out. I had pizza delivered, I made lemonade mix with gunky tap water. Later in the day, I unwound my bandages and saw the damage to my feet. My soles are two griddles of blisters, the cuts along the tops of my feet are criss crossed from the biting leather straps. I pour hydrogen peroxide over my feet, and brace for the sting. Actually the sting feels good. Hobbling to the front porch, the tide has surrounded Miner's Rock and is now receding. I sit and gaze, admiring the impressionist colors of pink and smoke gray.

I kind of wish I had a cigarette. I quit smoking, but every once in a while, I get the craving. Breathing deep really helps fight off the urge, so I relax my shoulders and exhale.

Candy was right, watching the changing tides and light on Miner's Beach is kind of like the best TV. Except it's real. It keeps changing. It's never the same. The view of the water, the rocks, the moon, the distant lighthouse, the changing of the tide,—it's all a show. The Big Show.

My eyelids are heavy, so I let them fall. I'm thinking of nothing, when there's a knock from the porch steps. My eyes pop open, "Yes?"

From below I hear, "Hello Marcia dear, It's me. Yoo hoo!"

Behind her cat-eye sunglasses, the realtor, Betty Ross is poised on the uneven sand wearing bone-colored low-heeled pumps. Her face is set with a mission, beaded with sweat, glasses steamed. "Betty!" I motion to greet her from my chair. "I'd come down but my feet are pretty torn up!"

She pulls herself up by the railing, carrying a large purse and a case. She's wearing a yellow print cotton pleated skirt and matching jacket with a twinkling broach, a silk yellow blouse with a bow at the throat. Hardly beach wear. Her pleats are so sharp you could shave on 'em. "Not to worry my dear! I'm fine."

Betty arrives on the porch and in the most ladylike fashion, takes a seat. Removes her glasses and wipes them on a handkerchief. "Now my dear, I heard what happened to your nephew. Is he all right?"

"Austin's okay, thank God." My head flops to the right. My feet are throbbing, but at least I don't feel pain.

"He was very lucky." Betty is serious, "a number of children have drowned in that hole over the years."

"Really? No one said a word to us."

Solemnly nodding, "Oh yes. Sadly yes."

"Well you know, Mrs. Briggs was the one who alerted my brother to look in the what is it, they call it a mine? . . ."

"Good for her."

"But imagine. If she hadn't said anything . . ."

"Tragedy."

"You know Betty. No one told us about that hole."

"I'm sure your sister-in-law knew."

"She didn't say anything."

"She should have known." Betty Ross smiles kindly, "That hole should be covered up!"

"It should. It really should."

The waves crash, a baseball game drones from a faraway radio. I'm sickened by Betty's laissez-faire attitude about the hole. Unmoved, Betty begins to look around, "High tide."

She must be thinking about refreshments. "Betty, I'd offer you a cold drink but we don't have refrigeration or ice . . ."

Betty gazes at my bandaged feet and insists, "Don't be silly—you stay. This is my opportunity to inspect the place. It's been quite a while since I've been here."

She stands with poker-straight posture and opens the screen door. In her wrinkled left hand she carries a stately Louis Vuitton case. She closes the screen door quietly behind her. Her footsteps cross the floors, the mini-frig door opens.

Waves build and release, build and release, I see Jack Junior and the twins building a sand castle. Much activity, shovels flinging sand, dutiful twins pouring buckets of sea water into the moat. They are happy.

Maybe Candy's right, this old fashioned simplicity may be good for the kids. No Boardwalk tattoo parlors, fried dough, amusement park rides or arcade games. Just sun, water and sand.

Betty emerges carrying a tray. Two bloody marys with fresh stalks of celery.

"It's cocktail time!" she chuckles.

"Well, well!" I admit, "Just what I don't need, but I'll take it. I'll take anything that's served to me on a tray."

She sits and serves the drinks. Mine is ice cold. The lovely cold tomato juice fills my mouth, with only a hint of vodka. "How did you do this?"

Betty opens the insulated, velvet lined cocktail case, revealing stainless steel shakers, jiggers, strainers and silver olive picks. With a clever look she swallows an olive, and wipes her finger with a monogrammed paper cocktail napkin.

Sitting primly, she swallows, ready to talk business. "My dear Marcie, you're right, the conditions of the cottage have really deteriorated."

"Yup." I hiccup, and laugh off my embarrassment with a long sigh.

"I am soooooo sorry." She looks as though she actually means it.

"Well, funny thing is . . . I'm the one stuck in this house of horrors with the kids and I can't walk."

"Where's your husband?"

"Everybody's at the hospital." I let my words trail off. I see my discontent click in Betty's eyes.

"Help!" I shrug, eyebrows lifted.

Betty poises, "Perhaps, if I may, suggest an alternative for tonight, at least."

"The hotel's full. Sleep in my SUV?"

"Marcie—you remember the Australian woman renting my house—The Curtis House—the one across the way? She has agreed to let you stay with her."

"Really?" *There is a God! A God with a weird sense of humor, but still, a God.*

"The house has plenty of extra room. She's only using the third floor. Her children and boyfriend have left. She's doing errands now, but I have the key. I explained your situation to her and she offered her first and second floor. Want to take a look?"

"Thank you! Give me a minute." I grit my teeth and dust off the sand above my ankles. I pull white cotton socks over my bandages, and slide them into the soft relief of a pair of Ugg boots that I'd brought along, never thinking I'd wear them. Keeping an eye on the sandcastle development, which seems to have the kids riveted, I limp across the sand to The Curtis House. As we climb the porch stairs, the deck wood is smooth and gleaming. Betty unlocks the front door, "Central air conditioning, so you can cool off, my dear," we enter the living room and I'm hit with a glorious wave of cold, sheer relief. *Isn't it lovely?*

Betty comments, as she floats through the rooms. The windows are huge and modern, the floors are bamboo wood with thick sectional rugs and gorgeous black leather sofas and loveseats strategically placed for the best views of the ocean. The kitchen, all stainless steel appliances and richly carved custom wood cabinets. Miles of swirling marble countertops with comfortable padded full seat stools casually strung around the islands. A half bath and a full bath down stairs, and without hesitation, I blurted out,

"Why didn't you rent us this place?"

"I'm so glad you like it!" Betty preeens.

"No I mean it. Why didn't you?"

Betty's smile drops. "Well, your sister-in-law insisted on Beach Rock and Red Rock Cottages."

"She did? Why?"

"Because her family stayed in those cottages long ago."

I shake my head in agony. *That Candy*. She didn't even try to explore the possibilities of other rentals.

"Let me get the kids, I'll be right back." I hobble to the front porch, waving my arms and calling the children to join me. I limp back into my new Dream House.

Betty has clicked on the television. "On the second floor, you'll find four bedrooms and two full baths. Fresh linens included. All I ask is you stay on the second floor. Leave my tenant her privacy on the third floor."

"Fresh linens?" Tears spring. I dab my eyes with a nearby Kleenex.

Betty raises a finger of warning to her lips, "Remember—"

"Privacy!"

"Total secrecy."

"About what?"

"About *who*. She is Giselle Dallarusse, a very famous Australian actress."

"Oh my God, really?" I smile excitedly. While I don't have the slightest idea who she is, other than an exhibitionist cock tease, I love the idea of celebrity.

"Let's keep her name between you and me, okay Marcie?" Betty is deeply serious, her eyes, a mandate.

"Don't worry. I've never heard of her."

Betty smiles, "No? She's won best actress at Cannes. It was a few years ago, granted, but . . ."

"Really? Why is she here?"

Betty reminds me of a character from an old black and white movie. "Miss Dallarusse wanted to be in a place where she wouldn't be recognized. Unexpectedly, she and her gentleman have had a falling out. She sent her children and Nanny back to New York and she is broken-hearted."

"That was her Nanny? I thought it was her mother."

"No, her Nanny."

"Well where is she now?"

"She's in Boston," Betty laughs and turns, "at a spa."

My kids arrive breathlessly, and erupt in cheers when I tell them the news. Betty and I instruct them to fetch our bags from next door, which they gladly do. After rinsing the sand off our bodies under the outdoor shower, the relief of central air envelopes my skin as the children fall hypnotized by Sponge Bob Square Pants on the gigantic TV screen.

35 Am I Dreaming?

I was kind of shocked to see Uncle Jack at my side when I woke up for a second. I thought it would be my Mom or Dad or Maddie, but I guess they went down to get something to eat. But Uncle Jack's face hung above me like a wavering hologram, he was saying, "I'm sorry Austin, I'm so sorry."

Then he kind of started crying, like super quiet-like. But I sort of felt bad for the guy, so I said, "Oh Uncle Jack. It's gonna be okay."

Then I fell back asleep.

36 Guilty Pleasure

My guilt over Austin receding, I leave the hospital and drive to a new, far greater source of guilt awaiting me at The Four Seasons.

I toss my bracelet in the glove compartment.

She's sitting on the love seat crying, when I walk into the suite overlooking the Public Gardens.

"I thought you'd be happy to see me," I smile calmly and kiss her on the head. I've just left a hospital ward where people have been crying for weeks over their children's inert bodies. Gwen's eyes are pretty darn clear for someone who's been reportedly crying for days. She hasn't even asked why I was at Children's Hospital.

"What took you so long?" she sobs. I turn toward the bar and pour myself a bourbon.

In my sternest Asshole Voice: "Gwen, you know where I've been. I've been on vacation with my family. We talked about it many times. And I told you not to call me, and to stay in New York. Does any of this ring a bell?"

Quiet as a little mouse, "Yes. I guess so."

Gwen is tactically braless beneath her tiny white camisole. The length of her legs is emphasized by the short silk boxers she wears belted with a satin ribbon.

Looking at Gwen makes my dick hard, so I take a long swallow of bourbon. I sink my hand beneath the ribbon. "Mmmmm. Forgot your panties, didn't you, Gwennie?"

She smiles coyly. I laugh, insert my hand and run my fingers over her hairless pussy. "Freshly waxed. Very nice."

She giggles, carefully balancing her reaction between shyness and white-hot desire. I can see the pale outlines of Gwen's rosebud nipples under the thin fabric. I put my bourbon tumbler on a coaster, kneel on the carpet next to her, pull up the lace edge of her camisol to reveal her genuine 34C's. Ahhhh. They are so pendulous and perfect. They fill my hands as I cup them from underneath, sucking each nipple, feeling them harden against my tongue, as Gwen breathes raggedly. "Oh Jack . . . . oh Jack I missed you so much . . . My two fingers enter her. She's wet and ready . . . Uhhhh! Jack . . . . !"

Her whole core snaps into an arc as my fingers twist against her g-spot. She convulses as I tease her clitoris. Clearing her voice, "Uh Jack . . ."

"Shhhhhhhhhh! No talking."

I stand up, step away, and exhale. I take my bourbon back. I relight my cigar, stare at her bare breasts. The silence is nice. This is the way it should be. I smoke my cigar, just looking at her mane of dark hair, her spikey eyelashes and red toe nails.

"Looks like I'm gonna have to fuck you." She giggles. I'm pulling off my shorts when she says, "Jack? I've been thinking."

"No thinking allowed." The tip of my cock brushes against my t-shirt.

"Let's talk Jack." She kneels, attempting to stop me with her little toothpick arms.

"Just let me fuck you." Her eyes close, and she relents.

I smoothly pull her down to her knees on the thick carpeting. I slide her boxers to her hip bones. "Jack, this is important."

I laugh, and push my cock into her mouth. I love looking down as she services me, her delicate tanned shoulders. Her mouth softly enfolds my cock, wet and hot, such pleasure, such relief as her left hand gently kneads my balls, as her right thumb and finger create a tight ring at the base of my cock. *Ohhhh Gwen is so good at this, it's a problem.*

Watching my cock go in and out, in and out of those perfect lips. I'm moaning and sighing when my dick indicates it's time to move south. As I push her flat on her back, I put my mouth over hers and insert my tongue. She tries to say something but my tongue muffles her.

She turns her head to the side, struggling, her hair is like a blanket of dark satin. "But Jack, I mean it."

"I mean it too," indicating my cock, "Here comes the Jack hammer."

37 Relief at Last

The Australian Woman has the third floor master suite to herself. Jack Junior, the twins and I overtake the second floor front adjoining bedrooms with a huge bathroom between them. Our bags and boxes and flip flops fill the hall with disarray. We don't care. The kids and I are so happy to be in a normal house with bathtubs and color televisions, my worries have melted away. My feet rejoice as they sink into the carpets. Joy is how I feel. *Joyful.* I bathe the twins in the giant size tub, they wash their naked Barbie Dolls' hair. Jack Junior sits in my bedroom, on the king size bed, watching a *Malcolm in the Middle* marathon. The other bedroom has three single beds, perfect for the kids.

I've tenderly removed the bandages from my feet—the tiled bathroom floor is cold and lovely, smooth and clean. The twins splash, turning the Jacuzzi jets on and off. At the sink, the cold water runs. I raise my right leg, put my feet into the instant relief. I left my left leg, put my foot into the sink, get another blast of relief. The lacerations extend from between my big toes into a V-shape across the top of both feet, deep and red. Irritated and itchy. And getting crusty. All of the tough skin on the pads of my feet is gone. My toe nails are cracked. But it's all so much better than it was before.

Where is Jack?

38 Rita Hayworth Lives

I stare at the ceiling.

Gwen is twenty-four.

I met her when she was twenty-two. I picked her up at Nell's one summer night. I'd never been to Nell's. But I was representing this young hot-shot screenwriter and he'd had a big win in Court. That's where he wanted to go. It was all business 'til Gwen swung past me, so sure of herself, so hot.

The minute I saw those Hollywood eyes and grin, I knew I had to have her. She was recklessly drunk, wildly beautiful, flirty, and had the eyes of every man in the place. She looked like Rita Hayworth. So I had the bar tender send over champagne to her circle of friends, I went over, introduced the screenwriter, then myself, got them all shit-faced and I afterwards, I walked Gwen home. She let me kiss her on the cheek. Which turned into a kiss on the mouth. Then a long, long hot kiss. Which led to me pulling her top down, revealing those amazing tits. Then I fucked her in the doorway of her studio apartment. It was very hot, and I'm not talking about the temperature.

The desire between Gwen and I has always been that hot.

It was easy to keep my infidelity secret, with Marcie embroiled in her car pools and fundraisers and Disney Princess parties and little league pizza nights. Meanwhile, I enjoyed the utter and complete pleasure of fucking a 22-year-old girl.

Marcie believed I was busy with clients. Meanwhile, I wined and dined Gwen. I managed to avoid every "event" photographer and seemed to encounter plenty of "near-misses"—people on the NY social circle who knew me to be a married man.

I let my luck, and my cock lead the way, and took Gwen for a few weekends at a secluded Hamptons resort. We lounged in a Jacuzzi, naked on the private balcony, my hands cupping her breasts, my cock in her pussy as the full moon rose. It was all blissful. Life was perfect.

And then, Gwen took a little peek in my briefcase. She came across a program from Jack Junior's school play in my briefcase, and she figured it out. She searched whitepages.com and found out I'm married with three kids. Wearing her most expensive pair of four-inch, black patent leather heels, Gwen kicked me in the shins about twenty million times, crying, screaming at me, dumping a vase of roses on my head. She slapped me across the face, kicked me out of her apartment and told me to never contact her again.

'Course I tried to call her a million times to apologize, but she changed her cell phone number and bounced me out of her email. She got a new job and left town.

And while I agreed with Gwen's every move, for her own sake, for her own future, life was hollow without her.

It was just as well. After all, it was Christmas time. And without the distraction of Gwen, I could focus on the kids, be a real Dad. I even fucked my own wife more often! And I felt better, because the affair had been a constant reminder of what a selfish bastard I really am.

I am.

But I missed her.

Then on New Year's Day, I got a call on my cell phone from Mount Sinai. Gwen had attempted suicide with Oxycondin. Serious shit. How'd they get my name? My cell phone number was written in pencil on her Social Security Card.

So in a sketchy explanation of an office emergency, I left my Marcie's mulled cider and maple popcorn balls and a house full of relatives and raced to Gwen's hospital room. Her eyes were like dark universes, so distant. She was skeletal. Sick pale. That beautiful, zizzling party girl, overflowing with enthusiasm, excitement, hope was officially gone. I saw what I'd done to her.

I ruined Gwen.

Tried to blame it on an overactive cock, which is true, *but still.*

And despite establishing a firm understanding that things were never going to change, I would never leave Marcie and kids, we cried, we agreed, we made a pact, we would be together, but things would never change . . . . here Gwen is—a year and a half later—trying to make me leave my wife.

Gwen's eyes have changed. They're hard. They're dealer's eyes.

I changed Gwen's eyes.

So in an implicit circle of guilt that can never be assuaged, Gwen forces me to the Boston Four Seasons, to rehash the same old argument for the millionth time.

"Jack, leave her!" she implores and cries.

I say nothing and stare at the ceiling, thinking of Jack Junior, crying and asking me, *are you and Mom together or not?*

39 Rich Girl, Poor Girl

Mrs. Briggs and I go back to grade school together in the little red school house on Old Mill Road, and while I admire her pioneering spirit, she is an abysmal landlord and even worse, a meddlesome property owner.

Yes, she and I did wear our pinafores to the Baptist Church Fair and ride the makeshift roller coaster. We were best friends.

To Gloria Briggs, I'll always be "Poor Betty!"

During the Depression, when my parents rented the Curtis house on Miner's Beach, my mother and father both Post Office workers, the both passed away from what I now assume was cancer, a perplexing disease that the times were not equipped to remedy. Gloria Briggs' parents showed their piteous honor of our friendship by legally giving me the Curtis house, in which to raise my two younger brothers.

Gloria and I shared our secrets, hoping boys would ask us to have a sundae at the Brooks Pharmacy ice cream counter, or invite us to a movie at The Wintusket Playhouse Theater in the Harbor. My façade was revealed to her every evening, as I washed my brothers clothes in an old-fashioned agitator mounted in the bottom of the tub.

She wore beautiful cable knit sweaters, helping me hang the clothes on the line, urging me on with encouragement, making me despise her as she went to the beauty shoppe for curls, going to the prom as I sat with my brothers the whole long night watching the moon rise, and as she held a party after the dance, to which I was not invited, to watch the couples in their long gowns and proper suits dance to a string quartet on the beach before Miner's Rock, I made a vow to myself then. And it burned and burned. As she saw me sew our pieces of clothes together, as I served canned food donated to our sad family from the GAR Hall, and all of the pity, the unrelenting pity, that descended upon us, wave upon wave upon humiliating wave. Lice upon our heads, discovered by the school, our heads shaved. There is no greater humiliation than that.

So when she and her family gave me the house, I had no intention of making it a "camp". I made my house a place that would win top dollar. And make her feel ashamed. As she did me.

Meanwhile, I wait, and wait, and wait, as she wastes away, not knowing the billion-dollar property she sits upon. And as the tides turn, the tides will turn in my favor.

But she's long gone mentally, looking upon her tenants as folly, me, as a long lost adjunct family member. It's been years since she and I had had lunch together. But how can I lunch with a crazy woman in pajamas?

40 *From the Frying Pan*

We stayed in the Ronald McDonald House last night. This morning, we're in our fresh clothing and comfy shoes. Richard seems more relaxed, and Madison is just happy to be with us, out of that "flea circus," i.e. Beach Rock Cottage. I'm just feeling a bit happier, for the first time, when Doctor Smith arrives. "Austin is out of the ICU."

"That's great."

"Yayyyyyy!" Madison cheers.

"Where is he?"

"We moved him to room 237. You can visit him soon. Mr. and Mrs. Grant, may I have a word?"

Richard looks around, "Sure. Where to?"

"Right around the corner, here have a seat." We step into an empty lounge with a coffee machine and a tray of cookies. I pour myself a cup and nibble on a cookie as Dr. Smith reviews his chart. Richard helps Madison pour herself a cup of hot chocolate. "Let me do it myself, Dad!"

"Now Madison," I say calmly. "Your Dad's just trying to help." The cookies on the table call to me.

This cookie is so buttery, I have to have another, just to figure out the recipe. Vanilla. A couple tablespoons of orange juice? Lemon zest? Obviously, butter. But how much butter? Probably a quarter pound.

Dr. Smith looks up, "Madison, I need to talk with your parents alone, so if you would go sit with your brother, I'd appreciate it."

Madison pouts, looks hurts as she turns toward me, helplessly. Richard and I exchange a look of *uh-oh*.

"But I want to know what's going on!" Madison's head presses against my arm. Her chapter book drops down against her knees.

"Honey, go visit your brother," I order, worried about what the doctor is going to say. Madison pouts and shuffles off clutching her book.

Knitting his eyebrows, Richard crosses his arms and leans forward. "What is it?"

"Richard and Candy, we need to talk. I've reviewed Austin's chart and done some thinking . . ."

"Thinking? I blurt.

"Mrs. Grant. We've run a lot of tests, and there's sugar in Austin's urine. He is about eighty pounds over weight—"

I have to stop him. "Oh, but Doctor, no disrespect but he's *big boned, it runs in my family*—"

I swallow the last of my cookie, dusting the crumbs from my lap, as Richard remains silent. The doctor exhales.

"Mrs. Grant, there are certain ratios between bone density, skeletal structure and muscle development. Austin's weight is more than his body's structure can handle."

I try to interrupt, but he won't let me, raising a palm.

"Hang on. I see early signs of juvenile diabetes, and I have to wonder what kind of damage the extra weight is doing to his joints, his back, his feet."

Who the hell does this guy think he is?

Richard is staring at me, silent. The doctor is paging through his papers. "I see that you and your daughter are also overweight, Mrs. Grant."

"Excuse me?" My mouth is open.

"You're obviously overweight."

"I beg your pardon????" I'm aghast. "That's none of your business and we're here about Austin, not—"

"I'm simply pointing out that weight is a family issue."

"Well you don't decide what my family—"

"Don't take this personally, Mrs. Grant."

"I'm taking this very personally."

"I have eyes. This accident occurred because Austin was stuck in a hole. His hands, feet and body are covered in contusions because he wasn't strong enough to pull himself out. He weighs more than his physical structure is capable of managing."

"That's not what happened—"

Richard's eyes slice mine, "You weren't there."

"I'm simply reviewing the facts, and I recommend a radical change in your family diet."

I stand and reach for my purse. "Come on Richard. Doctor Smith, I thank you for the advice, and I'll take it from here with our family pediatrician . . ."

I turn to Richard, "Let's go."

Richard doesn't move. But he speaks.

"Candy, Dr. Smith is making more sense than Doctor DelVecchio ever has."

I smile under Dr. Smith's glare. "We're going."

Richard doesn't move. Removing his glasses, Dr. Smith remains still, "Mrs. Grant, no one likes to hear this stuff. Especially a mother."

Tears dripping on the floor, I stand. "You'll have to excuse me." I head for the door, my face pounding. I avoid all eyes.

"Candy," Richard has never spoken to me in such an icey tone. He stands and points to a chair. "Sit down." Humiliated, I turn and sit, face burning.

Richard continues. "Doctor DelVecchio would never be honest with you about the kids' weight because most of his patients are overweight!"

"Richard!?"

"Honestly, he if were truthful, if he insisted kids eat right, he'd lose his practice!"

I plead, "Richard, this doctor isn't familiar with Austin's medical history."

Richard yells, "This doctor knows when he sees a kid in trouble!"

Richard's admonishment echoes and I'm mortified as a nurse down the hall stops and turns to look at us. Richard asks, almost eagerly, "How is Austin's heart? Is it healthy?"

I recoil at Richard's ridiculous question. *Austin's heart?*

Dr. Smith puts his glasses back on. "We'll know more after the tests."

"What tests?" I ask.

"Austin and Madison will be tested for Type 1 Diabetes, and Mrs. Grant, you should too."

41 One Way Ticket

Gwen's weeping hard. I roll to the other side of the king size bed and light my cigar. "Geez, will you cut the crying?"

She fans the smoke away, seething, "You miserable, egocentric pig—"

"I am, Gwen, I am." I let go a long sigh and stretch my arms across the bed. I try to take myself out of this misery, gazing out the window. The Swan Boats and passengers enjoy their simple, happy lives. I wish I were a swan. Except they mate for life.

Gwen pours herself some water. Standing next to the bed, her ass is like a tulip, fresh and pink. "Listen to me Jack. I can't wait around, wasting my best years on you."

I puff on my cigar. "You're right! You shouldn't! So don't."

"You're damn right I shouldn't!"

"Do me a favor. Go get a Kleenex and blow your nose."

Still naked, Gwen patters to the bathroom and slams the door.

I know what she wants. She wants plenty of money. She wants a chocolate lab puppy, and great big house in Chappaqua. She wants a princess-cut four carat diamond ring, catered parties and engraved invitations. She wants to pick out wallpaper and paint a nursery.

I know I'm not going to change my mind, and to keep on going with Gwen isn't fair to her.

I hear Gwen taking a shower. I yell over the din.

"Come on Gwen, let's go."

"Where?"

"Let's get out of here."

After a few minutes, she comes out, running a comb through her wet hair.

"Pack up, you're checking out of here." I'm dressed, collecting my wallet, sunglasses, keys. I even start whistling.

Gwen smiles, "Jack! Tell me! Where are we going?"

"You'll see." I don't tell her that I'm driving to Logan Airport and putting her on the next plane to New York. I don't tell Gwen that I'm never going to see her again.

42 Heathens

It's Friday morning. Both houses are suspiciously empty, so I walk through to take a look. Dirty dishes in the sinks, unflushed toilets. *Slobs! No manners!*

Even if my kin were hospitalized, I'd have clean sinks and made beds even if I had to do it myself, but that kind of housekeeping is long gone, long gone. I pick my way down the stairs, to find the Police Chief standing at the foot of Beach Rock Cottage.

"Good Morning, Mrs. Briggs. Gavin O'Healey."

"I know who you are."

"I wonder if I may—" He's squinting in the sun, holding papers. I eye him suspiciously, "What's this about?"

"May we sit down some place?" He's as fat as Paddy's pig.

"If you say so, but I've got plenty to do and you're holding up my day."

"Sorry Mrs. Briggs but I tried to call, couldn't leave a message so I . . ."

"Those newfangled machines are a ridiculous waste of money." I bring him into my house, shutting the door to the front sitting room. My son sleeps on the sofa with the TV going. His foreign wife feeds the mixed race baby with her breast, right out in the open. No manners. None.

"Mrs. Briggs, I've been asked by the Town Fire and Police departments—"

I remind this peon with whom he is dealing. "Gavin O'Healey, I recall the day when we relied on a bucket brigade to extinguish a fire."

"I understand that, Mrs. Briggs."

"Well?"

"This is an invoice from the Town of Wintusket for emergency rescue services rendered this past Wednesday night."

I grab the bill, put on my reading glasses and review this thing. Ambulance, Fire truck, three police cruisers . . . *Ten thousand dollars?* But I say nothing.

"I thought I should deliver the bad news myself." Gavin parries.

"Why am I being billed for a beach accident?"

"It happened on your beach."

"Our beach." I huff.

"Times are tough. The town doesn't have the money to pay for services on your private property."

"I open this property to the public on behalf of the town."

"And the Town is grateful, but not responsible."

"The Town has an odd way of showing its appreciation."

"The Town has absorbed over seventy-five thousand dollars in emergency rescue fees on your property over the past five years."

"So?"

"So we can't keep doing it, that's all."

"Why not?"

"We don't do that for any other resident."

"No other resident offers a beach."

"But you see Mrs. Briggs, things have become more complicated. This is all about money. And insurance. The days of the Town paying for accidents on your rocks, your end of Miner's, essentially, your property, are over."

I get up, adjust my bathrobe. "Okay well then. We'll just see about this. I'm calling my lawyer." My hands tremble as I shuffle through the Rotary Club phone book. I start to dial.

"Mrs. Briggs, Attorney Folds died three months ago."

"Oh. Guess I better find a new one." My head is spinning. "You can go now."

43 Liar

I'm in a first class seat on Delta's non-stop flight from Logan to LaGuardia. The flight attendant left me a bottle of champagne after he noticed I was crying. "Keep it, honey. Here's a pillow."

When I fell in love with Jack—I—I didn't know he was married. He lied to me. And when I found out, it broke me. Changed me. My world of possibilities shrank down to a wooden existence. Before, I had a life of love and excitement. The best of everything, the freshest flowers, the finest hotels, everything. I had Jack to myself. Or so I thought.

When I discovered he'd lied and he had three little children, I'd unwittingly become an adulteress. A shame I'd never deserved. I thought he would make things right. Leave his wife. I'd welcome his children into our marriage.

But he didn't make things right. Come to find out, he won't.

I uprooted myself, trying to plant myself in another life, and even though I gave it my best, I always found myself dining with another eager man, begging for my attentions. But I only wanted Jack.

It was like the rest of the world was living in color, and I was in black and white. And then, after a New Year's Eve celebration at the Waldorf, with a man who's name I can't even remember, I'd drunk too much and didn't care. He wanted me to sleep with him. I couldn't sleep with anyone after Jack. I couldn't even do it to avenge Jack, that's how badly it hurt. But after a wrestling match, I got out of the room, ran onto the elevator and waited for a cab outside. The hotel porter attempted to wave down a cab, and there I stood, watching car after car of happy couples wisk by, off to personal celebrations of their own. How could I not cry? I cried and cried, as every taxi passed me by. The Spanish concierge, going off-duty, gave me a ride to my apartment. Of course he tried to come up, tried to kiss me, but I sent him away.

Inside, the heat was off in my apartment. I climbed into bed, and downed the bottle of Oxycondin I'd been keeping in my bedside drawer, specifically for this type of occasion.

Despite my attempt, I lived.

Jack made me promise that I wouldn't bring up leaving his wife.

I thought I could change his mind, but now I know I cannot.

I should have picked myself up, dusted off my bootstraps, and found another younger man. But now, none of those men want me anymore because I am bitter. I am used goods. Unknowingly, not understanding how much Jack would or could steal from me, I stupidly spent the best of myself on him.

Back at Logan, before I walked through the airline gate to New York, Jack well-meaningly tucked two thousand dollars into my purse for cab fare, and with my acid eyes, I stated, "Cab fare? Or for services rendered?"

44 *Reassurances*

Dad is still not here.
Where is he?

Mom's feet are okay now, the twins are asleep. I'm not asleep. I hear a clock somewhere going *tick tick tick tick tick tick tick tick* really fast. My mind is marching forward to the beat of the clock, and I begin to wonder about the same thing I always wonder about.

I wonder about Dad and Mom.

Are they together?

Or not?

Dad kind of leaves us on our own. And when I show him a picture I drew in art class, it's kind of like he says something like "Oh wow!", and then I find my picture forgotten on the kitchen table.

We're alone tonight and I know Dad doesn't know where we are. Mom told me she couldn't get his cell.

Dad never told me I had to be the man of the house, like the Dads in movies. My Dad doesn't tell me anything at all.

All he does is go away.

45 Winning

I'm laying awake in my bed at the Ronald McDonald house. Out the window, I watch the cars belt down the road, off to their destinations. And for the first time in a long time, I feel good.

Madison is sound asleep in her cot, clutching her stuffed animal. Candy pretends to sleep in the twin bed opposite mine, her body's dark silhouette as mountainous as a football player's.

After years of marriage, today we had our first fight, and I won. I won because this was the first time I ever stood up to her.

46 Losing

The plane lands, and suddenly, the voice inside my head *that I never listen to* reminds me I don't have to live this life anymore. I don't have to be this prisoner for another moment. I can change my lot. I realize I have two thousand dollars in my purse. And I have a choice, which I shouldn't waste. I take a cab to my apartment, and begin to pack. I call my cousin in London and give her my cell phone number. She's letting me stay with her. I call my landlord and leave a message that I'm leaving town, and he's welcome to sublet my place. I'll be gone indefinitely.

47 The Daddy Wavelength

The Porsche glides along the Southeast Expressway. I don't listen to music because I have to get back on the Marcie-and-Kids-wavelength. I think about Marcie, her anxious blinking, and boney elbows sticking into my sides when she and I are brushing our teeth at the bathroom sink. Her force field of judgement and and . . . and . . . her never ending but totally justifiable mistrust.

Then I exit off 3A and zip along 228 south, past the regal antique homes of Hingham. Wonder if those guys mess around on their wives? Of course they do. All of us do.

I switch my thoughts over to Jack and the Twins. I think about playing with the Twins' little rubber duckies in the bath tub, how they've dreamt up a seriously complex story structure for the ducks, of offspring and marriages and adoptions and visits to the vet. Maybe I'll read Dr. Suess to Jack. Everybody's happy with me when I'm reading to Jack.

As I pull into the driveway, I see the beach house and wonder what kind of stories I have to come up with for my absence.

48 Regrets

The American woman and her children are asleep on the second floor. Her horny husband has been gone, thank goodness.

My forehead burns from the micro dermabrasion and acid peel.

These Americans. That horrible old woman. I am happy to be leaving soon. But now I am alone and I have the moon to myself.

The roof is mine. I take a bottle of champagne, cigarettes and a joint to the roof.

The roof has a Jacuzzi, I remove my robe and slide into the bubbling hotness.

I see Favrier in my mind. His dark hair in his wild eyes, his dimples and his big hands. His long, muscular legs. The gold earring. He is a shit, why do I let him in my mind?

I feel I am going to cry. I miss him. How dare he leave me this way? I gave him so much. So much time with him, wasted. For a woman, time is an investment. I invested my time in Favrier, and suddenly he realizes he is in love with me on vacation with my children. Mon dieu! He discovers this is serious! And then he is on the next plane to Paris. Fine.

I am due three child support payments from Marc, but he refuses to pay, claiming insolvency. The New York apartment lease is up in a month, and I don't think I can renew. How will I pay?

That fucking William Morris agent. Convincing me to move to New York. The agent claimed that "forty is the new thirty" and the "Australian cougar woman will be big hit in America." She promises me many roles, and I get auditions, even after a nude photo in Vanity Fair. Still no offers, no roles. Nothing!

I pay for the Nanny, the mobile phone, the cable and wifi and heat and water and all of these things, waiting for Marc's check every time I open the mailbox. And it is not there, that lousy sonofabitch.

And Marc claims he has no money. Ha! And the New York family court judge believes him. Corrupt. I am sure the judge has been turned by Marc's influential friends. The Judge ignores facts and only sees Marc's celebrity.

Marc has a mansion in Bedford and a summer house in Bridgehampton. A pied de terre in Soho. The judge believes Marc's sob stories.

Liar!

Why did I marry Marc? I could have married two of the Rolling Stones, but no! Stupid me! I married Marc, the businessman. The media mogul and art collector, thinking it would be a safer bet. What a mistake, what a mistake!

Forty. I am forty. Without a man.

Favrier owes me nothing. He has paid for this rental house. But why did I stay here, in this silly little town?

Because Favrier insisted on privacy.

I should have *insisted* on the Hamptons or at least The Vineyard! At least I would have been invited to parties! I would have *appeared Hamptons Magazine* or *Boston Common.*

Mistake upon mistake.

49 Rebellion

That spoiled, pompous little Lord Fauntelroy. All these years, I gave Richard a beautiful home. Freshly washed sheets with fabric softener! A lot of women skip fabric softening. I don't! Morning glories planted from *seeds* twirling up the trellises, fresh baked blueberry muffins baked from scratch! FROM SCRATCH! Don't I get any credit for going through labor twice without an epidural????

I gave up my career in public relations to be a stay at home Mom, driving a mini van to dentist appointments, girl scout meetings and little league baseball games. And of course I'm not the svelte woman I once was—I gave birth to two children! Give me a break! *He doesn't appreciate all the things I do!*

I can't sleep. Tomorrow, they're releasing Austin from the hospital and then we have to get tested for diabetes. No wonder I can't sleep. I feel like a fool. In front of the doctors. Staying at the Ronald McDonald house. The sirens of Boston, the flashing lights, the nightmare of all this.

50 Panic Attack

I park the Porsche and go into the house. It's like a blast furnace inside. I take off my shirt. Don't see Marcie around. Don't see her handbag. Can't hear the kids. Don't see a note anywhere.

I start looking all around for Marcie and the kids. I don't see them on the beach. While I'm wondering what's going on, I'm still relieved not to have to face Marcie. I go upstairs to the buzz of flies and thick, still air. No one. Suitcases gone.

Wait. *Has she left me? Have I been that much of a shithead?*

I call out. "Marce . . . It's me? Marce? Marrrcie?"

My voice just disintegrates in the hot still air. I go all around the crummy house, find myself stupidly opening the closet door again with the fifty thousand fly swatters. God damn it.

How'd she find out I've been cheating on her? She hasn't had a look at my cell phone lately. The cell bills go to my office. I pay for everything on my business Amex Card . . .

Back downstairs, I pour a cup full of Jack Daniels and walk to the road, attempting to call Marcie's cell phone. No signal. I shut my phone and walk back to the cool of the porch. I sit. Coming from the luxury of the Four Seasons, this place is like a Guatemalan sinkhole.

I don't blame Marcie if she left me.

Has she left me?

Did she find out about Gwen?

Did morose Madison spill the beans to Auntie about a phone call from Gweneth Paltrow?

I'm thinking . . . I see a Ken doll jammed under a chair. I pick it up, and his head falls off. I grab a flashlight from the window sill and walk over Beach Rock Cottage. No one's there. The only house where I see lights is the Australian woman's rental.

I try again, "Marce? Marcie?"

Fucking A. Now all I can think about is Australian woman kneeling naked on the beach, sucking that guy. My dick wakes up a little, even though he should be dead to the world.

I look at my phone. No signal, of course. Looks like the Aussie's the only one home.

Maybe she knows where Marcie is. Maybe I can get her to suck me. Hey, as far as I'm concerned, suckin' ain't fucking and eating ain't cheating. I walk over to her house and go up the steps. I ring the bell and wait. My dick is worn out from Gwen but it still leaps at the thought of Giselle. My mind's eyes can still see her slick tits reflecting moonlight . . . . I ring the bell again. How about I'll say I need to use her phone, which won't be a lie? I turn and look at the water. *What will she be wearing? Maybe just a thin robe? I hope not. I'm in enough trouble as it is.*

I turn when I hear the door, and *surprise, surprise!* It's Jack Jr. opening the door anxiously. "Dad! You're here!"

My dick goes soft as I hide my shock, and squat to be face to face with little Jack. "Hey Junior! What are you doing here? I been looking for you! Where's Mom and the twins?"

"We're all here Dad! The realtor lady said we could stay here, at least 'til Mom's feet get better."

He pulls my hand into the living room, into the relief of central air conditioning, "Look Dad! Plasma screen! Hi def!"

I look around the glowing interior of this swank beach cottage, what a turn of events. *My family's inside the Aussie's house!*

"I been looking all over for you guys! Where's Mom?" I'm surveying the framed prints and the smooth bamboo flooring. *Where's Marcie? What kind of face will she be wearing? Her "You've-Let-Me-Down-Again-Jack" face or her "Three-Giant-Glasses-of-Pinot-Grigio" face? Wonder if the Australian chick is here. I can't believe this luxurious house is next door to those two dumps! Why for Pete's sake didn't Candy rent this house?????*

"Come on Dad!" Jack races up the stairs. I follow, taking in the detailed railing and the hand-painted ceiling.

Jack's eyebrows are raised with excitement. "That's where we're sleeping! You and Mom are in here!" He drags me into a spacious, all white bedroom where Marcie lightly snores. Jack and I jump on the bed—"Marcie honey! I've been looking all over for you guys!"

"Jack," Marcie croaks. Her feet are sticking out from under the sheet. They're wrapped in dirty gauze.

"It's me honey," I shake her shoulder. "Hey Marce. I found you guys . . . What the heck are you doing here?"

I realize I'm laying on a King Temperpedic. Total relaxation passes over me as I melt into the mattress. Now this is a real vacation house.

"Dad, look! There's a TV in here too! And they got wifi here! And Dad—they got video games! Just like home!"

"Honey! Wake up!" Geez, Marcie's out cold. Her mouth is wide open, her arms wide open, she's wearing a t-shirt and sweat pants. Not exactly Victoria's Secret.

Jack is wired, bouncing up and down. I've got to figure out a way to mellow him out. I ask, "Hey Junior, did you guys bring my bag?"

"Yup, it's here. And Dad, you should see the Wii thing they got here—"

"Jack, let your Mom sleep. Let's go downstairs."

Downstairs, Jack breaks open a bag of Double Stuff Oreos and pours himself a glass of milk, which spills all over the marble countertop. I even like the soft paper towels in this house, as I wipe up the spill. Here, everything is about two billion percent better. Jack and I sit on the leather couch and turn on the TV. Best all time movie ever, *"Animal House."*

"Dad! Dad! What's that guy doing?" John Belushi is creeping under the field bleachers, looking up girls' skirts. Best I can come up with is, "He's doing research."

"What kind of research?" Jack looks at me in all seriousness.

"Medical research."

"I don't get it." Jack looks confused. It's midnight.

"Look, eat your cookies and drink the milk. We're going to brush your teeth and put you to bed."

"Nooooooooo! Dad?!?" He crosses his arms, pouting and stomping his foot.

"Come on, it's late."

"No."

"Listen Junior, you need your rest so you we can go fishing in the morning."

Magic words. "Okay Dad!" He squeezes my neck. I forgot what it's like to carry him. He's long and gangly but light as straw.

He opens his mouth wide and I brush his teeth with Spiderman toothpaste. The twins both sleep face down with their knees pulled up under their chests. "Okay Jack junior. Now go to sleep."

"But Dad . . . I'm not tired!"

"Yes you are. You just don't know it."

"Will you sleep with me?"

"OOOOOOOhhhhh . . . Okay." I lay down next to him. His mattress is just as soft and new as the other. He skootches over, his boney knees dig into my back, "Okay Jack, nighty night." I put my hands behind my neck and close my eyes.

"'Night Dad." Jack turns over. His foot is tapping. His fingers drum.

"Jack. Stay still."

"Dad I can't sleep!"

"We have to sleep. Have to, if we're gonna go fishing tomorrow. We just gotta get in the right frame of mind. Think of a cloud."

"Okay. I'm thinking of a cloud." He puts his arms behind his head and looks at the ceiling.

"Close your eyes. Think of a cloud that's made out of cotton candy, and it's got a roller coaster that has racing cars for seats."

"Yeah! And you can ice skate there."

"Plenty of ice skating." His hands move to my shoulder. He squeezes my bicep.

"We can ice skate and eat pizza and stuff like that." Jack whispers.

"And toast marshmallows." His grip on me lightens as he fades.

"Pizza. With no pepperoni."

And then, he's asleep.

I am not. The only sound is breathing children. I lay there. My toes keep flexing, a sure sign I'm wide awake. Without disturbing Jack, I gently slide out of bed. He sniffs a little, rolls into the warmth of the spot I've vacated, and goes back to deep breathing.

I return to Marcie. She is still sound asleep. As I lay down alongside her, I notice a half-full wineglass next to a bottle of Percocet on the bedside table. Well, well, well. Marcie's out for the night.

I lay there and wonder where Giselle may be, and in a demonstration of indomitable strength and virility, my dick salutes that thought. He orders me to get up and "cherche la femme."

No harm in just looking, right?

In the hall, I tiptoe, my head swivels around corners. The only other doors lead to beautiful cedar closets and a bathroom with dual sinks, golden marble everywhere and a huge mosaic on the wall. I go down the exotic driftwood-bannistered stairs. God, this place is nice. As I explore the first floor, I notice there's a small rear deck. Out there, I find a Rubbermaid trash barrel container, an outdoor shower nozzle and steps leading down to the beach and a blue dinghy turned over in the sand.

I go back into the house. Would the Australian woman be in the pantry? She doesn't strike me as the domestic type. Looking ahead to the stairs, I look up and—fuck me, there's third floor to this fucking place! *She must be up there!* I turn to take the next flight of stairs.

"Dad, what are you doing?"

I slam on my brakes and feign a yawn. "Jack! Junior! What am I doing? What are you doing!"

"Dad you woke me up. I heard you creeping around."

"Come on buddy, let's put you back in bed."

"I'm thirsty." His eyes are half-shut, but his feverish brain is still on high.

"Okay, okay . . . ." I grab a bottle of water from the fridge. Evian water. That Australian Woman knows what she's doing.

"Come on! Let's try this again." It's past midnight. I'm missing my shot at the Australian Woman. *Cherche la femme.*

Holding my hand tightly, Jack climbs into bed and presses against my side. His arms are around my neck. "Dad?"

"Just close your eyes little dude, and stay perfectly still."

"But Dad?" He wriggles around, his elbow just misses my eye.

"Jack we can't go fishing tomorrow if we stay up all night."

"Yeah, I know but . . . Are you still mad at me about Austin getting stuck in the rock?"

"Ahhhh, Jack. No. I'm mostly mad at myself. But no, I'm not mad at you."

"You're not?"

"Nope. I figure you'll never let something like that happen again."

"I won't! I won't I won't I won't." He smiles victoriously and exhales.

"Good. Now go to sleep." I run my hand over his head, his silky hair. He snuggles against my shoulder, readjusting, wiggling until he's still and he's eyes shut. Then his eyes pop open with another thought.

"Dad?"

"What????"

"I was wondering about something."

"What? Dear God, Jack what now?"

"Never mind."

"Oh don't say that! Tell me."

"It's okay. It's nothing."

"Jack it's not nothing! Tell me!"

"Okay. But don't be mad at me."

"I won't."

"I'm afraid."

"Don't be afraid. Just ask me. It's okay."

"Okay."

"Okay."

"Okay. Dad?"

"What?"

"Are you and mom together, or are you apart?"

A long wave of panic pierces my inner chest and rolls across my ribs, radiating.

"Why do you ask that?"

"Cuz you're never together."

"Oh come on. We're together."

"Really?"

"Really."

"You and Mom are together?"

"Yes we are together. Your Mom and I are together."

His body shudders against mine, as he bursts into tears.

"Oh Dad, I'm so glad you said that."

He cries all over me, water just gushing from his eyes onto my chest, my neck, he snuffles, I wipe the snot from his nose with my fingers, and my tears mingle with his, until we both fall asleep.

51 Offer refused

The sun hits me like a drill. I turn over, trying to sleep some more, but my mouth is pasty and my brain rings. Then I remember where I am, at the Australian woman's house, and I sit up straight.

My feet don't hurt so much. The good night's sleep did the trick.

Where is Jack?

I get up, hobble to the bathroom mirror and my eyes are ringed with mascara. I wash my eyes with cold water. It feels good. I brush my teeth and hair, then tenderly mince into the children's room. The twins are still asleep, tangled in sheets, their little red mouths open, their hair, tangles of curls. But what I love, is Jack and Jack Junior, glued to each other, little Jack branching all over his dad, Daddy Jack flat on his back, snoring away, his five o'clock shadow rough and his hair a mess of frizz. His feet stick out off the side of the bed. I lean down and kiss his lips. His eyelids flutter, "Hey." He smells of sweat.

"Hey. It's me." I know I don't smell much better.

"It's you." His eyes are slits, but I still love the color of his eyes, pale green.

"Where've you been?" I ask.

"Sleeping. Where've *you* been!"

"Here!" Come on." I take his big hand, and lead him into our bedroom. I whip off my t-shirt, his eyes go immediately to my tits. He holds them and grins. But I want sex. I get down on my knees, I look up, but he's backing away, "Wait . . . Let me take a shower . . . Need to wash up . . ." He turns for the bathroom door. Sticky, smelly, he doesn't usually walk away from this offer.

"Hold that thought!"

Outside the bathroom door, I turn the knob, it's locked. I knock. "Jack, do you know how rejected I feel right now?" I hear him peeing.

"Shhhhhh! I'll be right out!" Flush.

"Jack I'm sick of being turned down by you!"

"You're not being turned down!" The shower water blasts. "We're just always busy!"

"It has been so long since we've had sex—"

"That's not true, Marce!"

"When was the last time?"

"You remember! It was . . . it was . . ."

"You don't even know and that's not like you Jack."

"I'm washing my cock right now, rinsing . . . . getting all clean and ready to fuck you . . ."

"There's something going on that you're not telling me!" My whole mouth turns into a great big frown and the tears begin.

"Will you cut it out?"

"Why did you lock the door, Jack??"

"Stop it! Everybody'll hear you? I pull on my robe, find the Kleenex box.

"Why do I have to keep asking you for sex?"

"Marce, stop, I'll be right out!"

"You're making me feel like a fool!" The water stops, he opens the door, he's wet and clean, smiling, with a towel around his waist. He extends his arms, smiling, "Ready? Why are you crying?"

"You know Jack, I'm sick of begging. Forget it."

"Hey, hey, stop it! *You're not begging!*" He's wiping the steamed-up bathroom mirror with a hand towel, checking his nostril hairs. He is oblivious to my tears and sniffling. Which makes me cry harder. "You're making me feel like I have to beg for sex." I grab more kleenex and blow my nose.

"I am?" He says it with so little genuine concern or sincerity, his eyes never wavering from his reflection, I turn away and exit the bedroom, shouting over my shoulder. "Never mind!"

52 Poor You

Austin's been released. The papers are signed. I'm carrying a bulging bag of prescriptions, bandages, pamphlets, an inflatable donut, a three ring binder and a plastic water bottle that says, *"Diabetes: Beat It!"* Austin's waiting in a wheelchair with an attendant, and I keep peering around down the parking lot ramp expecting to see our van driving towards me. *Where are Richard and Madison? They left to get the van like twenty minutes ago!*

It just figures that I'm still here, planted at the front entrance of Children's Hospital, feeling like a cheese, wearing the same dress I've been waiting for two days, as taxis, Lincoln Town Cars fly by when all I want to do is disappear. I put the bags down on a nearby bench, fish my cell phone out of my bag and dial Richard. It rings and Madison answers, "Hi Mom."

"Where are you guys?"

"We're trying to leave but Dad's wallet is in your purse and we can't pay the parking."

Why did Richard put his wallet in my purse? "Let me talk to your father." He gets on the phone.

"Okay, okay I know, I know. I forgot my wallet."

"Yes you did."

"I can't leave Madison in the van."

"Well I can't exactly leave Austin."

"Isn't he with a nurse?"

"Well yes but Richard–"

"Honey, I'm pulled over with the flashers on at the pay booth. I can't drive backwards and we're backing up traffic—"

"Geez Richard! All right! Where are you?"

"Level one. Just take the elevator off the lobby down to Level one. I'm waiting right there. And hurry."

"Fine!" I hang up. God damn him! Here I am, for the millioneth time, doing what needs to be done, while Richard just sits there. I get on the elevator and guess

126

who's standing there. The doctor from hell. Dr. Smith. "Hi Mrs. Grant. I thought Austin checked out?"

The doctor's carrying a briefcase, departing for the day. I was hoping to never see him again as long as I live. But I smile.

"Yes—we're delayed." I don't look at him. The elevator stops and six other people get on. A couple of skinny moms in skin-tight yoga pants, pony tails and hoodies, pushing strollers alongside their handsome husbands.

Dr. Smith puts a hand on my shoulder, and I pull back.

"You have the blood sugar monitors, correct—?"

"Yes, we have everything." My tone indicates how much I don't want to talk.

"Now don't hesitate to call me if you need anything," Dr. Smith nods and smiles. The elevator bell rings as it's about to stop on Level B.

"I won't," I snap.

Then right in front of everyone, as the elevator door opens, he violates every HIPPA regulation by saying aloud, for every stranger to hear, "You know Mrs. Grant, diabetes isn't the end of the world. Try to look at it as an opportunity. Lose weight, get in shape . . . it'll change your life!" He smiles, walks off and the elevator door closes.

In the stainless steel of the door, the reflection of my face is bright red. These people are staring at me. I just want to disappear. To evaporate. To die.

At last, the door opens and I get off at Level one, where Richard awaits, playing a video game on his cell phone. The van is a few feet away, Madison is inside, watching the DVD player. Cars fly around the van as they escape the parking lot. The worn out Mexican parking attendant looks at me blankly as I dig through my purse for Richard's wallet. Richard apologizes, "Sorry sir!" Then blamefully turns to me, "What took you so long?!"

I stare at him, "Me? You're the chucklehead who left your wallet in my bag!"

Richard stares and wags his finger in my face. "When we get home, there are going to be a lot of changes."

"Oh, you bet there are, mister," I tell him, and throw his wallet on the garage floor.

"That was rude," Richard threatens, shutting off his cell phone.

"Oh poor you, you actually have to bend down and pick it up?" I hiss. "Do you think you can do it yourself, or do you need my help?"

"Hey! Are you inferring that I don't do anything? I pay for that nice four bedroom, three bath with the pool—"

"Oh and I'm just the slave labor?" People are watching our shouting match. It's loud, but behind closed van doors, rapt in "Princess Bride," Madison fortunately doesn't hear.

"I hate you Richard!"

"Oh really? I hate you too! For renting those crummy houses! Turning our kids into diabetics!" Richard fishes through his wallet.

"Get in the van, Richard," I growl, open the passenger door and get in.

"We're not going anywhere." Richard declares, stands in front of the van. I stick my head out the window.

"Get in now."

Richard, "You listen to me—"

The garage attendant steps in, "Sir! You pay and go, fight at home."

53 Dads To The Rescue

The ride home from the hospital is weird. Very quiet. Mom and Dad are not talking to each other. Mom looks like a zombie. She stares out her window. Dad stares forward at the road. Madison and I watch *"Princess Bride"*.

On the bright side, I'm out of the hospital. I'm on a prescription to fight infection, but that's it. I think I may have even lost some weight. Madison is being nice to me. I guess my brush with death makes her appreciate me more.

When we pull in the driveway of the beach house, Uncle Jack and the kids all come running. Mom takes her bag to the house. She doesn't say anything to anybody. She doesn't even look anywhere but straight ahead. The twins, covered with sand, want to help me, but I'm used to my crutches and don't need a lot of help. So they run off. The bandages make me look worse than I really am. "How are you dude?"

Uncle Jack chews on his cigar, while Jack Junior approaches me warily, drops his head and says, "Hey Austin man, I am so sorry. Really."

"It's okay Jack."

My dad says somberly to Uncle Jack, "Thanks again for driving Madison."

Uncle Jack says, "Sure, sure. No big deal. Just glad Austin's okay."

My Dad looks around, "Can't say that I'd glad we're back at these shit holes."

And out of nowhere, the Crazy Old Lady appears. "I heard that!"

Uncle Jack and Dad twist around, as she approaches, shaking like a junkyard, in dirty pink slippers. "I ain't deaf!"

Uncle Jack is kind of amused, I can tell. But my Dad isn't. My Dad looks like he could bite her head off.

Old Lady looks up at Dad and Uncle Jack, handing them a piece of paper. "You don't like staying here? Well I'm not thrilled with you either. Get a load of this!"

"What?" Uncle Jack wonders, as Dad and he put their heads together. Dad slides on his reading glasses.

Crazy Old Lady hisses, "I expect full payment before you depart." Uncle Jack's eyebrows narrow, "Whoa, hold on there Mrs. Uh—Mrs. Briggs."

My Dad's eyes zip back and forth as he reads, "This is a bill from the town for Austin's accident!"

Her twisted lunch bag face smiles.

"Damn straight. And I'm not paying it. *You are.*" So then she waggles her way around, attempting a dramatic exit, but her cane gets stuck in the sand and she almost keels over. Dad and Uncle Jack grab her and pull her up. I step away. She looks confused, wiping her cotton hair out of her eyes.

"Listen, Mrs. Briggs. This invoice is addressed to you. It's your responsibility to pay it." Good old Dad.

"No! No!" she strikes back. "Your stupid kid, your fault!"

Uncle Jack counters with, "I'm an attorney, and with all due respect, *you're* wrong—"

"Okay Mister Hot Shot Lawyer!"

Dad's reading the fine print. "Unless there's a named peril clause, but that's for long-term rentals."

But the Crazy One isn't listening. "Facts are facts. Your kid got stuck. I helped you get him out. I ain't payin' this bill. *You are.*" And then she scuffles off, like a whacky contraption.

"Dammit!" Dad murmurs. "I'm not paying for this."

"Damn right, you're not!" my Uncle Jack agrees, hands on his hips.

"Thing is, she might have a point. Bodily injury." Dad knows his stuff.

Uncle Jack waves his hands. "But she provides the hazard! It's on her land. There are no warning signs, the hazard is uncovered."

Dad grabs his car keys. "Let's go to Wintusket Realty. I'll drive."

Uncle Jack shakes his head, with his asshole voice, "Hey, I'll drive."

But Dad mans-up with, "No, I'll drive."

54 Poof!

As I walk into Beach Rock Cottage, I feel massive. The porch floorboards bend underneath me. I hesitate. I take the stairs one at a time, sensing that they may shatter. I am a horror, a monster, a fatty nemesis of lard to my family.

Upstairs, I lay on the bed, listening to the waves and cries of delighted children. I wish I were dead. I close my eyes, wishing to disappear into sleep. I really wish to disappear altogether, just evaporate. Gone without a trace. Implode, explode, I don't care. Vanish! But it's hard for a 200-pound woman to disappear.

I stare at the ceiling. Daddy long legs have established webs in each corner. The white window sill paint is yellowed and peeling. They're right, Jack and Marcie. These places are dumps. It's amazing how blind I can be. My will is so strong, I see only what I want to see.

Looking beyond the imperfections and blatant inconveniences, I've been imagining my childhood summer here. I've been going back to a time when I was carefree, full of possibilities and, and thin.

I've just been a mess. A mess. My life is a mess. It's all a façade. I'm nothing but a fool. Nothing but a fattie making others fat, making homemade donuts and grilled cheese and giant cookies.

I am fat, my children are fat, I am endangering their lives, I am their mother but I'm killing them. My husband hates me and I hate him. We've spent almost fifteen years going through the motions. We talk, we make noise, we don't communicate. And the thing I really can't understand is why Richard's never said anything about this to me?

55 Road Trip

It's been a long time since Jack has been in a mini van, I chuckle to myself as he miserably shifts in the passenger seat and struggles to buckle in. "Got a GPS?" he sighs.

"I know how to get to the Harbor." I like being behind the wheel. It feels good to be in charge and away from Candy.

Jack twirls an unlit cigar between his fingers, "Take a right up ahead."

"I know!"

"Okay, okay. Geeze!" Jack's eyes are shrouded behind expensive sunglasses, but I know his eyes are drilling beneath the bikinis of the teenage girls walking along the roadside.

"Real or fake?" he asks.

"Huh?"

"Real or fake?" he insists, pointing at the sets of tits going by.

I steal a look at the girl he's obviously referring to, a girl with spectacularly large breasts held in the confines of a tiny tan bikini. She almost looks naked. "Real," I snort, "I mean, she's what? Sixteen? Not like she's old enough for implants."

"Oh really?" Jack dismisses me. "You'd be surprised."

"How would you know?" I wonder. "What, you're a school nurse?"

"No. But what a fun job that would be! Heh-heh-heh!" He pulls out his silver lighter.

"No smoking in the van."

His hands fall helplessly. "Damn! Rules, rules, rules."

"You clearly don't follow them."

He turns, "What?"

"Just sayin'."

His face still smiles, but it's not a real smile.

"What are you sayin' exactly, Richard?"

"Nothing."

"Take a right," he gestures with the cigar. "You've got something to say? Just say it."

"Oh I will."

"I mean, no need to be a pussy around *me*."

"Oh so I'm a pussy?"

"Actually pussies are more interesting than you are." Jack looks out the window.

"You would know. You've seen plenty of pussy in your lifetime."

"You're trying to tell me something . . . but you're too much of a pussy to say it."

Not reacting to Jack's intimidation, I pull into the realtor's parking space and slam the van into park. "Okay Jack. I think you're cheating on Marcie."

He turns and looks out the window, "That's none of your business Richie boy."

"Marcie is my sister."

"Okay well if we're talking about sex lives, when was the last time YOU got laid?"

I don't say anything. I get out of the van slamming the door, stomping to the realtor's office.

"That's what I thought," Jack laughs, lighting his cigar.

He isn't the least bit concerned, as he rolls up the stairs and bends his neck down to fit through the entrance.

The realtor's office is like everything else around here, decorated in sea shanty motif. I notice my hands are trembling. "Hi. Is Mrs. Ross busy?"

"I'll check." The college girl behind the desk gets up and walks down the hall. I turn and catch Jack staring at her ass. "Oops!" he shrugs with clenched teeth.

"Gentlemen!" shouts a commanding woman, almost as tall as I am.

A mannish woman, probably in her seventies, with glasses so thick her gray eyes are magnified ten times.

Jack extends his hand, "Hi I'm Jack White, this is my brother in law, Richard Grant."

"Delighted! I'm Betty. Come right this way!" She leans over to the college girl and whispers something. The girl nods and disappears behind a closed door. "I was hoping to meet you gentlemen. You have such wonderful wives!"

Jack looks at me and laughs.

"Thanks," the building seems too small for Jack, who is tapping cigar ash into his palm when Betty hands him a clamshell ashtray. "I hear your son is doing better," she sits behind her desk.

Jack and I sit in matching club chairs. "Now this is probably your last day in town?"

"Tomorrow," I answer.

"And we can't seem to avoid that crazy—" Jack attempts.

"What great weather you had this week!" Betty nods proudly, as if she were at the controls in the sky.

"We spent a lot of it in the hospital—" I struggle.

"Bet the week just flew right by!"

"Betty." Jack removes his sunglasses. "Cut the shit."

Betty blinks. "Excuse me?"

The college girl reappears with a tray of Bloody Marys. "Thank you Tiffany." She hands me one and although I'm not one to drink at this hour, I'm happy to suck it down. *Maybe from now on, I'll start drinking heavily.*

"Hey pace yourself, willya Richard?" Jack warns.

I suck the last of it down and feel my brain freeze in pain.

"Will you put out that stinking cigar," I tell Jack.

"Oh Tiffany? Please, bring me another," I call to Tiffany.

"Sure, sir," she nods. She's wearing low cut jeans and a short wife-beater, revealing a horizontal stripe of brown, smooth skin and hip bones. I feel my cock harden. Jack's eyes graze openly at her pussy as he adds, "Just don't want to have to drive your shit-faced ass home in your charming mini van."

Jack puffs and smiles at Betty, who's been carefully taking all of this in, her drink untouched. "And some lunch please, Tiffany."

Jack appreciatively studies Tiffany's progress as she exits. Betty clears her voice, "As I'm sure your wives mentioned, I'm not in a position to refund your—"

"Oh we are so beyond that—" Jack waves. "We're getting into law suit territory now."

"Whatever for?" Betty's face is quite serious as she leans back in her high backed office chair.

"Luckily, I'm a lawyer."

"Really?" Betty states, unsurprised. She looks to me and I nod.

"We're here because Mrs. Gloria Briggs just gave us this." I pass her the bill from the town. She reads it as Tiffany presses a fresh drink into my hand and Jack continues.

"Your client, Mrs. Briggs—"

"She's actually my oldest friend—" Betty's a tad cagey here.

"You represent her, therefore she is your client," Jack stands and begins to pace, staring at the floor, then the ceiling, "and your client has provided us with sub-standard rental houses, she has been confrontational and a loud-mouthed nuisance. Harassment. Disturbing the peace."

"That she has," I agree. "I need to see hard copies of our rental agreements . . . May I have them?"

Jack continues. ". . . None of which we can really do anything about, except post a warning on Craig's List—"

"You'd post a warning on Craigs List!" Alarmed, Betty passes me the two rental agreements.

"Oh that's the first thing we'll do." Jack's eyes twinkle as he sits again. "And we can sue Mrs. Briggs for failing to properly warn us about the life-and-death hazardous hole that my nephew fell into the other day. On her property!"

"These are pretty straightforward," I pass the rental agreements to Jack. "Standard stuff."

"Gentlemen, I understand your frustration, but it's out of my hands." Betty gestures, "Mr. Grant, your wife waived the opportunity to tour the houses and she signed both leases—"

Jack rises from his chair. "My sister in law didn't think anyone would have the *nerve* to rent out rat traps for three thousand bucks a pop!" Jack declares, and takes a swig of his drink. "Ours doesn't even have a regular size refrigerator! It has a goddamn black and white television—!"

Betty counters with, "Listen. I was just doing a favor for an old frien–"

Jack's on a tear, pacing, waving his cigar. "You're not doing anyone any favors, Mrs. Ross! It's like you're stealing from my pocket!"

I move my chair forward. "Listen Betty, we are not paying the town for my son's rescue. As the landowner, this is solely Gloria Briggs' responsibility."

Betty stiffly refuses to take the bill. "I can't get involved in this. This is really between you and Mrs. Briggs—"

"Objection!" Jack shouts. "You are acting as a real estate agent on her behalf! You take a cut of our rental fee! How much is your cut?"

Betty swallows. "Thirty percent." Her face is long.

"So you got a couple thousand dollars for posting on a free website and dropping some paper in the mail? Jack leers at her, incredulous. "What a racket!"

And although I do not really like Jack, I can't help but admire the way he's taking her to task. Jack laughs. "This pays better than the legal racket!"

Ruffled, Betty fights back. "Mr. White, I don't want to confuse the issue of the rental with the issue of the accident." Betty's not slow.

Jack sits back down and puts his elbows on her desk. "My point is, you blindly let my naïve sister-in-law rent those shit box fire traps without a word—not a word—about what kind of shape they're in. You don't warn us that our crazy-as-a-koo-koo-clock landlord will be harassing us night and day, reprimanding us if we use the goddamn garden hose! Dropping in at any time! Unnannounced! In her pajamas and slippers!"

"You should have said something, you should have warned us ahead of time," I add.

"But then nobody would rent the houses." Betty counters.

"Don't confuse the issue that your client has a legal responsibility to warn tenants about a goddamn hole in the rock that children get stuck in every year!"

"Well, not every year, but—"

Jack's on his feet and waving his arms. *"For a total of six thousand dollars—your client has us* batting flies, suffering from heat stroke, we're killing spiders, we're trying to keep the crazy lady out of our houses, we're trying to pull a child out of a hole in a rock, and then we're off to Childrens Hospital! *This was supposed to be a vacation!"*

"Uh, pardon me," Tiffany squeezes by my chair with a tray of sandwiches. I sink my teeth into a roast beef and cheese on rye. Jack chooses a ham and cheese. Betty just sits there thinking with her arms crossed.

"You're right Mr. White, and you have my sympathies. And I'm sure, from your perspective—"

"From my perspective? From *anyone's* perspective—we have been *ripped off!* Hell, *we* should be getting paid to stay in those rat traps!" Jack laughs.

Betty removes her glasses and wipes the lenses with a napkin. "Okay. You're not happy. I understand. But I'm telling you, there's nothing I can do. I can't refund your money."

Jack backs down a little. "Okay answer me this."

"All right."

"Why didn't you rent us the nice house, across the way?"

"The Curtis House?"

"Yeah. That one."

"That's my house." Betty preens.

"You own the Curtis House?" Jack is completely surprised.

"Yes." She's smiling.

"Now that's a nice house!" Jack thumps his palm down on the desk. "Why didn't we get that one?"

"Because Candy Grant insisted on Beach and Red Rock cottages. She was adamant. She didn't want to see anything else, talk about other rentals, so. There you have it."

No matter what, the discussion always comes circling back round to Candy, renting the houses without looking at them first. My stupid fat wife. I stand and place my empty glass on the desk. "Well at least you're clear on our intentions. We will not be paying this bill for Town emergency services. Come on Jack."

Jack shakes Betty's hand, "It's been a pleasure arguing with you. Kidding."

Betty rises from her chair, shaken but still pleasant. "Will you be staying at the Curtis House again tonight? Please do. Your son will be much better off"

"What?" I'm confused. "Staying where?"

Jack looks at me with a tinge of guilt. "Uhhhhh . . . Richard! I forgot to mention, I mean, *we* all slept at the Curtis House last night. *All of us did*. Marcy. Me. The kids. Yeah. Now that's a nice house!"

I'm still confused. "But I thought the Australian woman—"

"Betty here let Marcie, me and the kids stay on the second floor because of Marcie's feet and the accident and all—"

"Where did the Australian woman sleep?" I wonder aloud, staring pointedly at Jack.

"I don't know!" Jack shrugs and smiles innocently.

Sensing a blast of testosterone in the air, Mrs. Ross narrows her eyes and wags a finger at both of us, "She's staying in the suite on the third floor. And she's not to be disturbed."

56   You Weren't Supposed To Tell

Am I dreaming? Maybe it's all the drugs they gave me at the hospital. But it seems real. Jack Junior and the twins lead us to a strange house, across from our rental house. "We're staying here now Austin," Jack Junior reassures me, and races up the porch stairs. The stairs are smooth wood. Everything is new. Shiney. And when the twins open the door for me, the air is cold. I carefully slide onto the couch. The bandages on my elbows and back feel the cool press of the leather, my front bandages crinkle when I sit, sending shoots of pain. But I forget that when I notice the TV. A giant flat screen TV. "Awesome," comes out of my mouth.

"Hi def," Jack Junior brags.

"We get *Max and Ruby*," adds a twin.

"In color," adds the second twin.

Aunt Marcie, who I didn't notice, at the kitchen sink, agrees. "Isn't this nice? You're going to be much more comfortable here, Austin. It's nice and cool in here." She brings me a bottle of fancy water.

"Hey Austin, I'm getting my PlayStation stuff," Jack Junior disappears. Madison comes tearing down from upstairs, "Listen Bro, you're gonna love it up there!"

I can only nod. I'm kind of tired. Don't want to move. I just want to watch this TV and play video games. Aunt Marcie places a bowl of microwave popcorn on the coffee table. "Where's my mom?" I ask.

Aunt Marcie slides onto the couch next to me. "Your mom is next door and I'm just wondering, Austin honey, did something happen at the hospital . . . Something else maybe?"

"I dunno Aunt Marcie. Where the remote?" I wonder.

"Here." She passes me the remote, and opens my water. I click through the stations. "Austin, honey, your mom? Is something wrong?"

"Yeah. The Red Sox game is on, but I'd rather watch the Phillies."

"What?" Aunt Marcie stares at me with her laser eyes, her eyelashes sort of clumped together and she's tapping her fingernail on the table. Tap, tap, tap. She's not going to give up 'til she gets the information.

"Yeah, well Mom and Dad are sort of in a fight I guess."

"A fight? Over what?"

Why won't Aunt Marcie back off? "Yeah well, turns out when I was in the hospital, not the first one but the second one, the doctor figured out I'm like a diabetic and so is Madison and so is Mom."

"Oh my God! Really? Diabetic?" She leans back, her mouth open, her eyes taking in new thoughts.

"Yeah, see Mom didn't really want to believe the doctor guy, but Dad was like, all gung-ho. Dad agrees with the stuff the doctor was saying."

"Your Dad agreed with the doctor?"

"Yeah and Mom really thinks the doctor is wrong. So they ran these tests and sure enough, we're diabetics. Madison and I are, but Mom like *really is.* Like she's a super diabetic! But not Dad. Dad's not."

Aunt Marcie puts her hand on my head. "Oh my God, Austin, I'm so sorry."

"It's okay."

"It'll be okay, buddy. You'll see. It'll all work out." I hate it when grown-ups call me "buddy." It's so fake.

"Austin, Mom *told you not to say anything!*" Madison screams down from the stairs. Her face is twisted and her arms are folded. She turns and runs back up the stairs.

"Aunt Marcie asked me!" I scream back.

"I made him tell me Madison!"

Aunt Marcie stands and disappears upstairs to go wheedle more information out of Madison. Jack Junior still hasn't shown up with the video game stuff. I feel my eyes begin to close, and that's okay. But then the front door opens and there's that lady. The lady who, you know, was on the beach that day. That one.

"G'day . . ." she smiles behind her sunglasses. "Oh! It's you! The survivor!"

She's got a weird accent. She's carrying all these shopping bags. She grabs an ice tray from the frig, and turns to me.

"Oh you're looking fit and fiddle! No worries for you!" Her nails are covered with silver glitter, like Christmas ornaments.

"No worries," I mumble something like that. Her upper lip is shaped like a soft cushion, and I'm staring at her mouth, I guess.

"Well. You'll be comfortable heah, and I'll be up on the third floor. But don't come a knockin'! I need my beauty sleep." She swishes her hair all around, like ladies on TV shampoo commercials.

I shake my head no. She laughs, gathers up her bags, and goes up the stairs. She is wearing a very short skirt. Which, I'm not gonna lie, I kind of like. I can see under it, black lace. I remember her, on the beach, and my dick jumps. It's been doing that a lot lately. She's gone.

Just then, Dad opens the door, arms full of luggage, with my Uncle Jack right behind him. "Well well well. Will you look at this place!" Dad takes the room in, whistling,

"Bamboo. Nice."

"Yeah, it's really nice. Where's the Australian?" Uncle Jack asks me. His eyes are wide with expectation. He's curious about that Australian lady, that's for sure.

"Upstairs. But Uncle Jack, she said to leave her alone."

"Got it," Uncle Jack nods. "Of course."

"There's a third floor?" Dad puts our bags in a corner then runs his hands over the counter. "That marble? It's called Touchstone. Imported. From Egypt."

"Now this is worth three thousand a week," Uncle Jack pours himself a glass of liquor. Dad answers, "She must get five."

"Really!" Uncle Jack gulps. "Let me have the clicker," he orders, so I pass it to him. He clicks along 'til he hits a Yankees game.

"I'd say so, central air, right?" Dad gets a beer from the refrigerator, shaking his head. Posada's up.

"Infuriating we spent six thousand bucks between us to stay in those dumps when we could have both stayed here for less. Fuck me."

Dad never uses the F bomb. It's weird. It's weird that he's drinking. "Dad, where's Mom?"

"Your mother is resting in the other house, and doesn't want to be disturbed." He rolls his eyes at Uncle Jack, who chuckles and swigs.

"All the women don't want to be disturbed today." Uncle Jack drains his glass with a confused smile. "What's up with that?"

"What the fuck," Dad growls. "I thought we'd drive back to Jersey today, but no. She says she's the only one who hasn't had a vacation. So."

Uncle Jack shakes his head at the ceiling and smiles sarcastically, "Aren't you going to go comfort her?"

Dad finishes his beer victoriously, the glass edge hits the marble countertop with a ping. "Nope!"

57 Digging for Dirt

Cotton ball soaked in hydrogen peroxide, Aunt Marcie dabs at the disgusting clumps of snot-colored puss forming in her cuts.

"That's repulsive," I sniff and look in the mirror. Maybe I should get highlights. A lot of girls in my class have highlights.

"So what else did the doctor say?" Aunt Marcie has this big basket of nail polish, in like, every color. Even light turquoise.

"I wasn't there. The doctor gave us all these folders and books. We have to go on special diets. And we have to exercise every day. Stuff like that."

"Do you have to test your blood with a meter?" Her shoulders are tight and up against her neck. I open the bottle of turquoise and right away a drip lands on my leg. I wipe it off with a tissue, but it leaves a blue streak.

"Yup." Aunt Marcie's eyebrows go up. "But Mom says we're not going to start that stuff 'til we see our pediatrician at home. And *her* doctor at home."

"Makes sense." Aunt Marcie nods, but her eyes move around a lot as she thinks.

"Yeah. But now, Dad doesn't like our doctor at home." Aunt Marcie perks up when I tell her Dad's side.

"Oh? How come?"

"Dad says our pediatrician is a lying phony bastard and we should have been diagnosed years ago."

"Your dad might be right, but your Mom's feelings are hurt, I'm sure."

"Hey did you know Uncle Jack has Gweneth Paltrow as a client?" Aunt Marcie looks confused, then smiles.

"Oh yeah, your Uncle Jack has all kind of clients."

"He was talking to her on the phone when he drove me to Boston."

"What was he saying? I love the details about movie stars."

"I didn't hear it all, but he called her Gwennie. That's kind of cool to call a movie star Gwennie."

Aunt Marcie's face changes, just for a second, then she digs through her cosmetic bag looking for something.

"Hmmmm. So the diabetic thing. How do you feel about it?" She squeezes Neosporin into the cuts.

"About being a diabetic?"

"Yeah."

"Mom says she'll get me a Pandora bracelet if I keep quiet and go along with her."

"Really?" She winds a roll of gauze around her feet. "I didn't know you were into Pandora. I thought you were an American Doll girl."

"American Girl dolls are for babies." I keep messing up, so I wipe my nails off with polish remover. I love the smell like I love the smell of gasoline.

"I see. So I'll put Pandora beads on my Christmas list for you?"

"Yeah, or Tiffany key jewelry."

"You're a little young for Tiffany, Madison." Aunt Marcie's feet all wrapped, she slides them into her dark brown Uggs. She's so cool. "So where's your mother?"

"Mom just wants to be left alone."

"Don't we all?" Aunt Marcie smiles, and gingerly walks down the hall.

58 The View From Down Under

My mobile rings.

"Gisele honey, it's Rita."

"I thought you were dead. Abducted by aliens."

"Hah hah. Listen, I'm booking you for a *Showtime* role."

"Hold on there. What show?"

"That one about California?"

"Yayyyyyyyyyyyy! I love that show!" I can feel my face smiling for the first time in days. "When?"

"Wednesday. That gives you just enough time to get to LA. I have you booked on a flight from Boston tomorrow."

"Fantastic! Is this an audition or a sure thing role?"

"A little bit of both."

"I get it."

That means the director will ask an assistant and the assistant will tip-toe over and whisper, "they want to see you nude."

I imagine myself, stepping out of my dress. It's always fun to watch their faces. There is nothing more empowering than being naked in a room full of men. I love the way they look at me. And after that, I'll get the role. Just gotta make sure to keep it.

"I'll email you the audition script and all the details."

"Okay great! Where will I be staying?"

"Beverly Hills Hotel. Uh. Gotta go. I'll call you back. Bye!"

I place the phone on the side table. The afternoon sun is intense on my breasts but my nipples are protected with sun block. I want my underarms to tan, so I raise my arms over my head. I look down at my gleaming abs. A rush of desire passes through me. How I could use Favier's long hard cock right now! I resist the urge to touch myself.

The Jacuzzi is off, so the water is still and cooling as I slip my legs in. I splash my breasts.

If this job lasts the season, that will mean uprooting the kids from New York, which will inevitably send me back to Family Court. But I need the money. To pay the lawyer. So I can go to Family Court to get the six months of back child support Marc owes me.

Those American women downstairs have it so simple, and they don't know it. I pine for their lives of ease. Security. Prosperity. "I'll get out of here tomorrow," I remind myself.

Watching the families far below on the beach, men chasing after their sons, wives serving sandwiches, rubbing sunscreen on little shoulders, pouring lemonade, they all make me feel even more alone. I know what'll cheer me up! I'll do my nails.

59 Tete a tete.

The blonde naked Barbie tells the dressed, brunette Barbie it's okay to be naked on the beach. "That's not true, honey. You have to wear a swimsuit," I warn them even though I know they're just playing. I don't want them to get the wrong idea.

The twins look at me like, what, huh? "Mom! But that lady—"

"That was no lady," I laugh, filling a basket with cold wine, cheese, Carrs water crackers. "I'm going next door to hang out with Aunt Candy. Did you hear that, Jack?" I yell over the TV.

"What?" Jack, Richard, Austin and Jack Junior are glued to the TV screen. Madison's playing something on a lap top while the twins continue their soap opera. Honestly, the minute there's air conditioning, TV, wifi and video games, they're all inside the house. Maybe Candy had a point about "roughing it" at Beach Rock and Red Rock Cottages. At least everyone was outside. But here, at Curtis House, everybody's indoors glued to LED screens.

I'll tell Candy how right she is. That'll make her feel better.

"I'm going next door to talk to Aunt Candy. There's pizza and grinders in the frig. You watch the kids, okay?"

"Yeah, okay Marce," Jack replies.

The tide is high and lifeguard whistles shriek at sun tanned surfers. I mince past the circled beach chairs and towels, past Crazy Old Lady, who raises her arm, waves her stick at the kayak, imploring me to, "move that contraption off my land!"

"Move it yourself!" I yell back to shocked observers, as I tenderly climb the splintered stairs of Beach Rock Cottage. The screen door slams behind me.

The living room is dry bake, dust flakes spin among sun rays. There's nothing happening in the kitchen, unusual for a Candy environment.

"Who's there?" she calls weakly.

"It's Marce." I unpack the wine and cheese and set them on a cutting board. "It's just me."

"What do you want?"

"Oh Candy stop it. Come down here and let's chat."

"I don't want to chat!" Above, I hear mattress springs squeal as she rolls over in bed.

"You're not going to spend the last day of vacation hiding. You've been in here all afternoon!"

"Go away!" she yells back. Weakly.

"Candy! Just you and me. They're all at the other house. I'm pouring you a glass of wine." My voice rings with false cheer.

"Well, in that case . . . Give me a minute."

"I'll be on the porch." The screen door snaps behind me. Late afternoon shadows turn long and purple, as a pack of boys run, gazelle-like, along the water's edge. The chair I settle in has the strongest looking legs, gray wicker unraveling from the arm rests.

Jack would say the corkscrew is the busiest utensil in our kitchen, and he'd be right. The cork slides from my wine bottle effortlessly.

It's really not so bad here if you're staying in a comfortable house that is, I think to myself. This beach, trumps anything found on the Jersey Shore.

I hear Candy's footsteps. Anticipating Candy's arrival, I slice cheese and place the squares on the crackers.

With a rattle of the screen door, Candy emerges wearing an oversized sleeveless black T shirt with flowered capris and black flip flops. She got some sleep. Her eyes are clearer. Still a little swollen, but she looks better. Her long dark hair looks flat ironed. Nice. This is the best she's looked all week. She studies my mummified feet, encircling her fingers around a wineglass stem. "Well, well, well. Looks like you had one helluva pedicure."

"Hey . . . I forgot that you haven't seen my feet—I walked all the way from the salon to here . . ."

"I'm sorry I left you behind. But I *just knew*—"

I solemnly admit, "Candy, I should have come with you."

"—I just knew something was wrong with one of the kids. I just knew it! And thank God Austin's all right."

"A mom has to do what a mom has to do. Plus, your instincts were right." I pat the chair next to me. "Are you guys leaving today?"

"The last thing I want to do is drive back to Jersey and be told what a lousy mother I am."

"Oh Candy, cut it out, everybody knows that's not so."

"I have one more night here, the house all to myself? I'm staying." With a defiant grimace, Candy lifts the bottle and pours herself a glass, filling it to the rim.

"Crackers? Gouda?"

"Now Marcie. Don't steal my job as food pimp!" She whispers, and glares, not sitting.

"What?" I spread mustard on a cracker.

"I found out. My nickname," she states dryly.

"Candy!" I screw up my face. "What are you talk—"

"Jig's up Marcie. The good doctor at Children's Hospital dragged all the nasty details out of Austin and Madison and Richard. About food. And the fact that I'm killing my children. I got it all. Even my nickname. Food pimp." She sits with a thump.

"There's no nickname! Stop it!"

"Now, now . . . In return, the good Boston doctor, Doctor Smith—not the evil New Jersey doctors with whom I collude and plot and plan ways to kill myself and my children—"

"They said that?"

"Dr. Smith!"

"No doctor would accuse you—"

"Your holier-than-thou brother! Who sits at the right hand of the Father! Who weighs himself every morning and eats fiber cereal and does cardio–"

"Candy. Don't blame Richard." My wineglass is empty. I pour more. Good thing I brought the big bottle.

"Richard sided against me! With a strange, unknown doctor—"

"He's not some whack job. I mean geez, Candy, he's a chief doctor at Childrens Hospital in Boston!—"

"Still."

"*Sided?* You think Richard sided against you??"

"Your brother acted like I was a pariah, like I am a millstone around his neck and he's merely been tolerating me for all these years, as I do the scheduling, the driving, the scratching of his hairy back, the writing of the thank you notes, taking care of the kids when they're projectile vomiting while he snores away—" Her cheeks pink, her chins wagging, I realize how hurt and angry Candy is.

"Look—if it's any consolation—Richard has not said a thing to me about this." I gulp.

"Well that's Richard's style. Isn't it?" Candy's eyes crackle. *"He doesn't say a word!* He keeps quiet, never showing a card. Even if something is bothering the living shit out of him. He won't say a thing. *Until* someone *else* broaches the subject, and then Richard is a like a guest host on The View!!! He agrees and agrees with *them,* making me, i.e., *the wife,* feel like a fucking loser!"

The pieces are coming together for me now. In Boston, Candy wasn't just diagnosed as a diabetic. *Candy was humiliated.* She felt betrayed by Richard with his allegiance with Dr. Diabetic. Trouble is, I agree with my brother and the doctor. If Candy hasn't seen this day coming, she's been blind.

"Hey, getta look at that." I point to a huge catamaran dancing along the horizon, its orangey red sails radiating light.

Candy leans in, "Don't change the subject."

I lean back. "Look, men are wusses. They don't have the balls to say what's really—"

"Your brother's had a million opportunities to—" She's waving her hands, "—say *something!*"

I brush my hair back. "I'm not a marriage counselor! But—"

Candy leans in closer, "Your brother *could* have said—"

I comb out a snarl at the base of my neck, "Maybe he was waiting for *you* to bring it up—wasn't it obvious?"

"Me? Me? I'm the one who's doing everything *else!* I'm filling out the permission slips and making sure they floss and helping them memorize all the state capitols—! French verbs! Conjuctivitis! I do everything! You should have seen me at the hospital!"

Nostrils flaring, her face is beaded with sweat. The collar of her top is drenched.

"I'm sure you did it all once again, but Richard's the bread winner. It's the deal we made as stay-at-home-Moms, right?"

I lick my lips and turn away, to the hiss of the waves. And I wish I wasn't hashing this out with her, but it's almost like it has to be done.

"Oh I see what you're saying." Candy leans back in her chair and the wicker groans as she takes a long sip of wine. She puts her feet up on a worn out wicker ottoman, and I see the real toll her weight has taken. Her ankles are full of fluid. Kankles. Candy has kankles. It's sad because I remember when her legs were shapely. Slim. We'd dress up in high heels and short skirts, go out to the bars on the Ohio State Campus. She has scars from her bunion surgery on the knuckles of each foot, and her big toes sprout black hairs.

"You're implying I have nothing to complain about. Well, I could be one of those work moms, who take an hour to pick-up their sick kid from school. The work Moms who never volunteer for PTO. *They bring grocery store cupcakes for the bake sale!* They show up late for Family Night—wearing high heels on the gymnasium floor! Do you know how much it will cost the school system to refinish the school gym floor! Marcie, I know you know what I'm talking about! Those Moms who are so busy with their own lives, they aren't there when the kids need them—"

"Well shit Candy, no one could out-Mom you! What other Mom is psychic enough to hear a siren and know their son was stuck in a rock!"

"Damn right!" she grins triumphantly.

Then I lower my voice, "But it's okay to be one of the Moms the school secretaries bitch about. And take some time for yourself. Go to a pilates class. Did you say you joined Jenny Craig?"

Her smile goes flat. "Marce. Do not go there."

60 Cherche la Femme Part 2

At last. The moment I've been waiting for. The minute Marcie goes out the door, my dick softly begins to chant: *cherche la femme. Cherche la femme . . .*

I look around. Richard seems pretty into the game, although he's drinking his fourth beer, totally unlike the dude to booze it up this much during the day. But hell, the guy deserves a break.

The boys are gaming. Madison's on a laptop and the twins stand on high stools at the kitchen sink, playing with a bucket of hermit crabs and starfish. Everybody appears to be busy and the time is now.

I pick up my cell, cigar, drink and slide on my shades. "Goin' out for a smoke."

"Okay Uncle Jack," Austin answers.

I slide my way to the rear of the house, take a whiz in the half bath and silently exit the back door. Yep. The Aussie's Range Rover is parked out back. So she must be upstairs. Good. I light my cigar and explore the outside of the house. There has to be an alternative staircase to the third floor.

Gotta get up there. We're leaving tomorrow and I can't get that chick out of my mind. Gotta hit that.

Out on the beach, Crazy Old Lady is holding court. In her pink cotton wrapper, she yells at a bewildered woman about feeding the sea gulls.

There are clusters of hot high school chicks reclining on beach towels, their knees bent, their bikinis tiny. Nearby, testosterone trios of jocks play with a football.

Cherche la femme.

There's not a lot of time left. There's got to be a back entrance, some kind of fire escape. I walk all around the outside of the house. Nothing. I stand there thinking, puffing my cigar, watching this dorky guy out on the water, struggling with a windsurfer, pretty funny, actually.

I look over to the porch where Marcie and The Whale sit. The Whale is waving her hands around, she's swilling wine and crying, blowing her nose into a cocktail napkin. Marcie listens patiently. They look like they're very busy.

Good.

61 The Blind Side

The minute the door closes behind Jack, I know what he's up to. The difference is, now he has an adversary.

"Jack Junior!" I command. The boy looks up from the GameBoy he and Austin are sharing.

"Yuh?"

"Where's your Dad?" He looks around, to the spot where his dad just sat.

"I dunno," he shrugs.

"I need your Dad right now. Can you go find him?"

Austin protests, "Dad—"

Jack Junior looks around, "But Uncle Richard–"

I'm stern. "Right now, buddy. Go out and call him. I'll be back."

Jack Junior gets up, zooms out the door, and starts yelling off the porch, "Daaaaaaa-d? Oh Daddddddd!?" The screen door slams behind him.

"Austin, I just noticed there's an Xbox in the den!"

"Really?" He lights up at the thought.

"I think it has Brink."

"Awesome!"

"Go set it up for you and Jack Junior!" Austin reaches for his crutches and hops into the den.

Grabbing the remote, I click and click until I hit the movie, *"Girly Girls."*

All three girls' heads swivel to watch when they hear the theme music. *"All us girls together! Out here on the floor!"*

Where am I getting my courage, I wonder. I'm not nervous or shaky. For once, I know why I'm here and what I want.

Madison and the twins are oblivious as I grab two cold beers and race up the carpeted stairs to the third floor.

I open the door without knocking. On the third floor landing, a stone floor with a large, rustic wooden bench. Boutique bags, Giselle's expensive leather carry-all and a pile of fashion magazines. Branches of fragrant yellow honeysuckle are in vases in every corner. My feet sink into the small hand-knotted prayer rugs as I look around. There's an antique set of French doors. I pass through them, then turn back, close and lock them behind me. Past the massive living room furnishings, past the wet bar/kitchenette, a monstrous master bedroom with floor to ceiling windows. There's a side door of leaded stained glass. I open it to a bright copper spiral staircase. I mount the narrow steps, carefully, quietly, to a rooftop sanctuary, surrounded by high hedges. In the middle, a large round Jacuzzi. And naked, the Goddess.

I stay still for a moment, just looking at her. Her hair is back in a pony tail. She's laying on her stomach, her legs parted, painting her fingernails. Her buttocks so tight, her hairless crevices open and ready, the back of her legs, smooth and muscular. I clear my voice, "Uh, excuse me, Giselle?"

She lifts her head, turns, pulling a white towel over her body. "What?" She looks at me, unsurprised.

"I thought you could use one of these," I walk towards her, uncapping a beer. "Remember me? I'm Richard."

"Yeah. Sure. Well well. Isn't that nice of ya. Hot up here." She pouts and sits up, fanning her wet, sparkling nails. She accepts the beer, waving away my handshake. "Thank you."

I sit in the empty chaise nearby and uncap my beer. "You're welcome."

Below, I can hear Jack Junior yelling for Jack, "Daaaaa-d! Dad!"

She pulls the towel tighter around. "What are you doing here?"

I smile. "Bored I guess."

She doesn't smile back. "I thought you were told not to come up here."

"I hoped you might make an exception." It's with great restraint I don't reach out to release her hair from the ponytail.

"Bored you say?" She sips the beer.

"Just looking for something to do. Mind if I hang out here for a bit?"

She looks me up and down, lips open then tighten. My cock feels it. "Something to do, eh? Where's your wife?"

"What wife?" I smile.

She's suspicious. "Are you a cop?"

"Nope. Just a straight-laced financial manager who is very bored."

"Okay then." She slips on a pair of sunglasses, and from under the cushion, removes a joint. "Let's smoke."

Her long silver fingertips strike a lighter, and those pursing lips take a long haul. She passes the joint to me and I thrill at the prospect of putting my lips on something that just touched hers. I haven't smoked pot, in I don't know how long. I never really did, actually, not even in college. And that makes me more excited. I've never felt more alive as I suck on that joint, looking at her, letting the smoke fill my lungs. I hold the smoke down, pass the joint back, then erupt into a monumental coughing fit. She laughs a little as I shudder and hack.

"Drink your beer." That gap-tooth smile is so sexy.

I obey. "I'm okay. Pass that over."

She stays still, wearing an amused expression. I inhale a smaller amount and hold it down as long as I can.

It feels as if an invisible curtain has closed around us, separating us from the rest of the world. I pass the joint to her, but she shakes her head no. I take another long draw. It fills my lungs easily now, I hold it and feel even better. "This is good stuff."

I pass it into her twinkling nails and take a long drink. "Thank you."

"What do you want?" she asks me.

"Honestly?"

She shakes her head yes.

"Want to have you."

"Me?" She giggles.

"Yes. You and only you. I've never wanted anyone more." I gently reach for the edge of her towel, and softly, slowly, I begin to pull it away from her breasts. Where am I getting my courage?

I know what I want and I'm going for it.

She smiles elusively, and allows me to remove her towel. I'm drawn to her magnetically, as she gives me her private showing. Her large, perfect breasts with up-pointing nipples, her flat narrow tummy gleams beneath. My cock comes alive. "May I?"

Giselle nods. My hands cup her breasts, along the bottom. They're not fake. Like I saw her man do that night in the hammock, I tease her nipples, lightly playing.

She gets up from the chaise lounge, her hairless pussy inches from my face. The towel drops behind. Touching her hips, I bring her pussy to my mouth, like an oyster, and drink it in. It's clean and salty. My tongue circles her rosebud clit, and she shudders. I reach up for the magnificent breasts. She parts her legs further, allowing more access. She's wet.

Giselle drops to her knees, her sparkling fingers pull down my swim trunks. I pull them off as she gently kneads my balls. Her fingers are gentle yet firm. I lean back in ecstasy. She knows her way around. My cock is throbbing, she feels it.

"Come," she invites as she steps into the still Jacuzzi waters. The way she walks around naked, so comfortably and casually, her breasts bobbing, I could watch her all day.

She seems pleased at the size of my fully erect cock as I wade into the water, she leans over and takes my cock whole into the back of her throat. Her tongue and lips bring me larger and harder. Then she lets go. I dip and let the water drench me. Her hands grab my buns, her breasts inches from my chest, her lips inches from my lips. My hands pull her small round ass cheeks closer to my cock. My reaching cock rubs her pussy and her lips meet mine in a serious of soft exploratory kisses. Her nipples are hard against my chest. I reach under her arms, sit her on the side of the Jacuzzi and push my cock into her, her breath catches as she arches back. My cock goes all the way into her tight wetness and her cunt gives me a good squeeze. A perfect fit. I stop kissing her lips and go to her breasts, cupping them up to suck her nipples. She's fully aroused. I plunge into her again and again, and pull out when I get close to coming.

"Let's go," she swims out of the tub and walks dripping to the winding staircase. I grab my things and follow.

She doesn't care that we're wet and naked. She climbs on all fours into the bed, her ass in the air, like a beautiful stallion, her head turned, she waits for me to mount her. The afternoon light paints her. On my knees, I plunge my cock in and fuck her doggy-style. My hands surf the mounds of her ass and her shoulders. My fingers trace the deep plunge of her spine. Her breasts swing wildly as we fuck. When I feel my balls shrinking and hardening, I pull out again and lay on my back. She stays on all fours. "Spank me," she whispers.

My hands caress her bottom tenderly, even teasing her hairless anal opening, and then, with my right hand, I slap her.

She sighs, turns and smiles over her shoulder at me.

I insert three fingers into her pussy, and she moans with pleasure. I lay on my back, pushing my head between her legs, and I begin to tongue her clit, my fingers entering her pussy. Her breasts swing overhead.

I want this to last. Just when she's fully aroused, I say, "Let's take a break."

The ceiling is covered with a brass and blue mosaic of stars and sky. She lays on her side, her tanned, Sports Illustrated body displayed before me.

I can hardly believe this is real, but it is and I'm grateful it is. I wanted this to happen. I made this happen. I don't care about anything else.

"You're so at ease with your body," I comment.

"I've posed nude for Australian Playboy."

"Really?" She's not in the least bit ashamed.

"I was in Vanity Fair last year . . ."

"Nude?"

"Yes."

I note that I must get a copy. "You must sunbathe nude a lot."

"My favorite place is in Mexico, a beach called Zipolite."

"Let me take you there someday." *What am I saying? Candy barely lets me play golf.*

154

"You silly man," she smiles. "But I'm glad you came up."

"I am too," I whisper.

"I wanted to have sex this afternoon," she admits and lights another joint. "I'm glad."

"I've been wanting to have sex for five years," I agree with a puff of the joint.

62 Stuck With The Kids

What the fuck is this? Richard has taken off and I'm stuck in the house with the kids.

"Where'd your dad go?" I ask Austin who is hypnotized by Xbox. I wonder if he's supposed to have more medication or what.

"I dunno."

"Madison?"

"What?" Her eyes glued to the TV.

"Where'd your dad go?"

"What?" She's immersed in a parade of pre-teen girls in pink prom dresses dancing and singing.

"Never mind." I shake my head and sip my bourbon.

"Daddy, daddy, daddy we want macaroni and cheese!" The twins beg, so I get busy at the Viking gas stove. Among our kitchen items, there's a box of macaroni and cheese on the counter. I boil the water, find the butter and milk, all the while, I'm glancing out the windows, looking for Richard.

Where is he?

Austin, Madison and Jack Junior smell the food cooking and decide they want pizza. I switch on the oven, remove the cold pizza from the refrigerator and grab a stack of plates from the cabinet.

Richard's not with Candy or Marcie, he's not in here, he's not in his car, he's not on the beach. That's when it hits me, *I know where Richard is.*

63 A Man's Favorite Pleasure

"When was the last time you and Richard spent any time alone, if you know what I mean?"

"What do you mean Marcie?" Candy's suspicious. The conversation is going into forbidden territory. My voice wavers.

"Well, I know it's hard for me and Jack to ever get the time, but shoot, *I try to make the time . . .* time when I'm not the chauffeur, I'm not the calendar keeper, or the activities director, or the nurse, I'm Jack's wife."

"Geez Marcie. We're talking about your brother. That's personal."

Candy turns her head completely away and stares down the beach at the final vestiges of sunset. An errant football bounces off of another porch front, and spins along the sand.

"When was the last time you went down on Richard?" I whisper.

She turns back to face me, eyes aghast, "What do you mean, "go down"?

My words are quiet, so no one can hear. "You know, blow job?" This topic requires me to lean way forward in the chair.

Candy recoils. "Me? A blow job? I don't *do that.*"

Her distaste is theatrically demonstrated in every possible way, until I can regain her eye. No wonder my brother is so unhappy. She's made him into a unich.

"Candy, are you *kidding* me? You don't give Richard blow jobs?"

Her forehead an accordian, she primly shakes her head, 'no.' "No way. Isn't that what that filthy Bill Clinton intern did? What was her name?—"

"Oh come on, it's a man's favorite sexual pleasure!" It's true, *I mean it really is true. No wonder my brother seems so immobilized. He's not getting any.*

"Richard would never expect that." Candy is adamant, "Richard doesn't want me that way." But I'm shaking my head in disagreement.

How would you know? Have you even tried?"

"Why would I try that?"

"I dunno, to keep your marriage going?" I grin. "Sex is the glue."

But Candy's having none of this. "How about you Marcie, when was the last time you did Jack?"

I'm not self-conscious. "I went down on him the night before last."

"Really." Candy is searching the horizon, trying to rise above the subject of the conversation. She folds her napkin and sips her wine.

"That's pretty whorish."

I sit up straight. "Wait, and you? When was the last time you did *anything* with Richard?"

Candy's eyes are like needles. "That's none of your business."

I deflect her strike. "You know what Candy? You don't have to tell me, because it's obvious you and Richard don't have sex."

"None of your business." She reaches for a cracker and breaks it in half with her fingertips.

"Fucking would do both of you a world of good! Pick a weekend. A week! I'll watch the kids. Go to some place exotic, and—" Candy still won't look at me.

"Look Marcie, I've just found out that I'm not only a diabetic, I'm also going through menopause. So I've got other things on my mind right now, Marcie." A tears slips from the corner of her eyes down her cheek into her neck folds.

Long pause. Long, long pause. "So those sweats you've been having are hot flashes?"

"Apparently so." Candy keeps her profile to what's left of the sun, her eyes averted.

"So they did tests and—?"

"They did a lot of tests, and basically I have to change everything about the way we live, what we eat, what we do every day. The hospital gave me all kinds of meters and batteries and equipment, charts, pamphlets, DVDs. It's so *complicated*—"

"Oh Candy. You'll do it. You'll get *past* this—*I know you*—"

"We have to learn how to use meters. A nurse will be visiting us next week. And a dietician. Richard isn't speaking to me—"

"But maybe this is for the *best*—"

"The last thing I want to do is get on my knees and suck his cock," her empty wineglass hits the table a little too hard.

I wave my arms, "This is exactly the time when you *should!*"

"Richard would be shocked!" She turns her tear-red eyes to me. Fallen-faced, Candy looks like a Saint Bernard.

"He'd love it!" I gush.

"No. No, no, no. He'd be shocked because I've never done that before!"

"Never?" I narrow my eye. I can't believe her!

"Never." She giggles a little.

64 Like Bells

"Can I come in your mouth?" I gasp, as I kneel above her, pumping into her, her breasts rocking beneath my force. Her pussy is like a slip and slide it's so perfectly wet, and she groans with pleasure. My right hand works her clit as my left pulls her in and out. I'm urgent, desperate, "Giselle. I'm gonna come in your mouth."

"Okay," she agrees as my fingers finally hit the right spot. "There! Don't stop! Right there!" I work as she wishes, not too light, not too rough. Her legs stretch open wide, she's elastic and eager and a feast to the senses.

Giselle's back arches and arches, I feel her cunt muscles tighten and like a fantasy, she's orgasming beneath me. I watch her tightened face and she cries out again and again. I'm harder and harder and then, my orgasm hits. I bring my dick to her mouth and let it all go. Her lips are there, pulling and sucking all of it out of me. "Ahhhhhhhhhhhhhhhhhh!" Her mouth is around my cock, taking in my river of cum. And when there's no more left, as I expel my last breath, she swallows. And then, she smiles.

I fall on my side, she thrusts in the last aftershocks of her orgasm. We're still for a second or two.

And then she begins to laugh. A laugh from deep within her center, and it sounds like bells. Bells from sleighs and towers, tricycles, shop bells and cathedrals, the Liberty Bell and every bell in the entire Universe, celebrating. She laughs and laughs and laughs.

"Thank you."

"No, thank you."

65 *Quitting Quitting*

"I have a bottle of red in the kitchen."

"Go get it." Candy waddles through the screen door. I see a college kid on the beach with a cigarette. I get up and lean over the porch. "Hey! Hi! Hi! You! Yes you! I was wondering, do you have a spare cigarette?"

He comes over grinning. Tall, dark close cropped hair. "Lady, you want to buy this pack offa me?"

"Sure!" I grin, reaching for my bag, and I give him a twenty. "Got matches?"

"Take my lighter." The kid laughs quietly as he curls the bill into his low slung jeans and walks away.

Why do they wear their pants that low? They look ridiculous.

I sink into the chair lighting up, as Candy returns, shocked to see me smoking.

"Marcy! What are you doing? I thought you quit?"

"Oh Candy. Just quitting quitting for a night." I exhale a plume of smoke. That feels so good.

"You're a bad girl!" she chides, shaking her head.

"You think this is bad?" I laugh. She's brought out a big bottle of red Zinfandel. My handy cork screw takes care of the job, and I pour. Candy's so drunk, she falls into a chair. We both settle back.

The low tide and moonlight turn the beach blue and silver as seagulls patrol the shoreline, picking at clamshells. People walk their dogs as a lone kayaker skims along the horizon.

"I should go check on the kids." Candy burps.

"You know what? No. Let the Dads take care of the kids. You're gonna be dealing with a big hot mess tomorrow. So you might as well relax tonight." I light another cigarette.

"That's right," Candy agrees. "You know Marce, I been thinking 'bout what you were saying and—"

"Oh God. What was I sayin'?"

"About sex."

"Right right right. Sex. Sex is the glue."

"Well you know Marcie, I have to be honest. I kinda forgot about sex. I mean I didn't forget about it. It's just like, not on my list."

"Of things to do?"

"Right. I mean, we have so much to do, all the time, it's like there's no time!"

"I know whatcha mean. Hey. Whatever happened to that guy you dated before Richard. What wuz his name . . . he was that great big cute guy. Wasn't he a Sigma Ki U? Wasn't he an exchange student?"

"Oh I remember. Franz." Just saying his name makes Candy's face light up. "You used to like sex with him."

Candy's eyes look to the heavens, remembering Franz. "Boy I sure did."

"How come you guys didn't end up together?"

"Aw, he had to go back to Sweden. Where he was betrothed to another."

"*Betrothed?* Are you fucking kidding me?"

"I know. How fourteenth century."

"Betrothed."

"He was like some kind of Swedish royalty."

"So you didn't fight for him?"

"He sent me a plane ticket. Told me get my passport in order. Said he couldn't live without me. But by then, Richard and I were dating and I—"

"You didn't fight for Franz?"

"You make him sound like a country! Years later—I got an invitation to Franz's wedding. So I assumed it was too late, and I just sort of settled in with Richard."

"You should look Franz up on Facebook."

"Really? Oh I don't know how. You think I should?"

"You sure should! If we had wi-fi at this stupid house we could look him up right now!" I love sitting out here, smoking, drinking, not worrying about the kids and having girl talk. "It's so interesting the way we all sort of end up in these couples."

"It's all like musical chairs once you get in your late twenties."

"Tick, tick, tick goes the biological clock."

"I wish I'd chosen a different color for my bridesmaids dresses."

"I wish you had, too."

66 Daddy Duty

Richard peers over his eyeglasses at Excel charts on his laptop as I stick my head in his bedroom door, "Hey Richard. There's pizza downstairs."

"Oh no. I'm fine." He's got some kind of a spread sheet up on his laptop screen.

"Where you been, my brother in law?" Richard puts on a very convincing show of official business. Rearranging papers. Typing.

"Just busy. Hey. You heard anything from the girls?"

"They're over at the other house getting soused. They're on a bender."

"No shit. They're drinking?"

"Been through two big bottles of wine. Oh they will be hungover tomorrow."

"Well okay. Thanks for letting me know, Jack. I'll be down in a minute. See you downstairs buddy."

Richard can't wait to get rid of me. But I have to make him feel guilty. "Uh, you're not forgetting about Austin's meds?"

He leaps up from the bed. "You're right! Time for Austin's pills."

Richard scurries around, opening prescription bottles and finally he goes downstairs. Time for the twin's bath and brushing of the teeth. *Cherche la femme?*

67 The Truth Comes Out

"I know what I wanted to ask you," I remember, out of the blue.

"What's that?" Marcie asks. She's lit the wrong end of a cigarette and knocked over her wine glass, sure signs that she's hammered.

"What's the deal with Jack and that bracelet? Isn't it a David Yurman bracelet?"

Marcy's head falls back in mock frustration. "You really want to know?"

I shake my head at her. "Yup. He looks ridiculous with that bracelet."

"I don't care."

"Just sayin."

"Candy, here is the real story. You know how Jack won't wear a wedding ring?"

"Because it's uncomfortable?" I remind her of the cockimamey story she told me about why Jack won't wear a wedding ring.

"I asked Jack to wear the bracelet, because he wouldn't wear a ring. Just 'cuz I like some piece of jewelry on him, saying he's mine."

But I wonder aloud, "Why didn't you put something on him when you got married? I mean, why now? You gave him that about a year ago . . ."

"I know, I know I know. I asked him to wear it when an affair he'd been having for a long time finally broke up."

"An affair?" I'm not so shocked that Jack had an affair. Just shocked at Marcie's easy knowledge of it.

"Or so *I thought* it broke off. I guess she's back in the picture." Marcie shrugs, attempting to light the proper end of the cigarette.

I wave my hand in her face. "Jack's cheating on you? Who is she?"

Marcie leans back, her tattered feet rest on the porch railing. "She's beautiful. About ten years younger than me. Taller."

"You've seen her?" I'm gaping. My jaw is on the floor.

"Oh yeah. I hired a private investigator. He gave me photos. And she's amazing. Guess that's one thing to feel good about. Jack's not fucking around with some dumpy run-of-the-mill chick."

I'm thunderstruck. "Marcie, this has been going on for how long?"

Marcie drinks deep. "Doesn't matter. I have everything I need, if I have to take him to court. Meanwhile, I have my kids, the house. And my marriage. Not sure I want to ruin everything." She rolls her eyes, like I would understand. But I don't. "How did you find out?"

"Well Candy, you know how you had a feeling when you heard those sirens? I had a feeling. Jack wasn't grabbing for me in bed anymore. He wasn't trying to fuck me at all, and that was unusual. But of course, I passed it off as marital life, settling in. Then, one day, there was a book of matches on his bureau. From a resort in The Hamptons. Ordinarily, I would've forgotten all about it, except I got a phone call from that same resort, saying I'd left a pair of shoes there. So when Jack Junior was in school, and the twins were in pre-school, I drove up to fetch the shoes."

"And?" I'm astonished.

"They were black patent leather Christian Louboutin's. Size seven. Very pricey. They musta cost Jack at least five thousand bucks. My feet haven't fit into a seven since after I had Jack Junior." Marcie laughs.

I'm still shocked.

"The manager was surprised to meet The Real Mrs. Jack White. He kept apologizing and when I finally got him to talk, he showed me receipts. You can't explain away Jack's signature."

"No you can't." We both sit there for a minute. The tide, though low, is still active, white froth shooting out from the darkness. "I had no idea you were going through this."

"Well, I didn't want anyone to know." Marcie smiles pertly.

"And here I am feeling sorry for myself about being a menopausal diabetic." I grin and shake my head at my own selfishness.

"Aw Candy, it's gonna suck being a menopausal diabetic. I'm not gonna lie. But shit, you had to be in denial, to not know, all along, that you weren't heading for this!"

I don't protest. Marcie's on a roll.

"And shit! After all the times Jack cheated on me *before* we got married, I was a moron to think Jack wouldn't cheat on our marriage, and sure enough *he does.* You and I. We both have been incredibly (hiccup) stupid."

"You know what I'm getting from all this—"

"What?"

"Marcie. You work out every day, play tennis, get highlights religiously, get your nails done . . . You look amazing every minute of the day, and still, still Jack cheats."

Marcie sits up and does that black woman neck shift with the wag of a pointed finger, "Oh honey, all that beauty work ain't for Jack. That's for me."

68 Unbelievable

Can you believe this?

I'm doing clean-up duty in the kitchen. Richard is upstairs with all of the kids. They're watching *"Pirates: the Sequel of all Sequels."*

I'm the one washing the dishes and dumping the trash.

Out of nowhere, suddenly, the Australian woman sweeps through the living room, wearing a long skirt, flip flops, buttoning a loose jacket over her tank top.

"Oh hello. Jack is it? Just to let you know. I'm going out for a moment, don't lock the door! I'll be back in a little while."

Giselle is wearing silvery black eye liner and her earrings are long and jingly. I race after her. She's headed for her car. "Where are you going?"

"To the liquor store. Or the "packie" as they call it around here. May I get you something?" She keeps moving forward as I skip and gallop behind.

"The liquor store closes at ten and it's nine-fifty," I remind her.

"Oh dear," she pouts.

"May I drive you?" I grin.

"No, don't be silly."

"My car's faster—" I point to my Porsche.

Giselle eyes my car and changes her mind. "All right. Hurry."

"Sure thing—" I open the passenger door to let her in. As she lowers herself into the passenger seat, I catch a glimpse of her tanned, gleaming knees. "Hurry!" she pulls her legs in.

We go blasting off toward the Harbor. She turns her head away from me to look out the window.

69 At Last

The kids are asleep. Austin is medicated. The house is silent. And I have had the best sex of my life. I've cheated on my wife. Nothing will ever be the same, I'm going straight to hell, and I don't care!

Visions of Giselle weave through my mind as I run the spreadsheets on my computer. Everywhere my mind ventures, I'm not there. I'm on the rooftop. I'm three hours ago. Reliving it. Remembering the way she slowly revealed her breasts to me. Reliving her head over my cock. What I did to her. What she let me do. The way she made me feel. Like I've never felt.

This is life as it should be, I tell myself, as I stroll out to the front porch of Curtis House to the lazy overhead fans and sumptuous chairs and the surf rolling in . . . real sex . . . sex, unapologetic, pure sex, without shyness, without excuses or caveats . . . then I overhear pieces of Candy's and Marcie's conversation. They are loud and slurring. Totally drunk.

". . . I have everything I need to take him to court . . ."

A wave from the incoming tide washes out their words.

". . . he wasn't grabbing for me in bed anymore. He wasn't trying to fuck me at all . . ."

More waves, one after the other, tide coming in strong . . . .

"You can't explain away—"

"No you can't." Boom! Another wave crashes. Boom! Another wave.

"I had no idea you were going through this."

"Well, I didn't want anyone to know." Boom! The waves withdraw, sand being sucked from the depths. Then the explosion of another wave. Which reminds me of Giselle's lips . . . But then another wave crashes, and I hear.

"And here I am feeling sorry for myself . . . ."

I can't tell one voice from the other. Dear God what are they talking about? The best thing for me to do is go upstairs and go to bed.

70 Oh Brother In Law

"I have to ask you something."

"What?" Giselle is impatient with me, a lift of one brow.

"Why'd you fuck him?" I demand.

"Who?" She draws her neck back.

"You know perfectly well who." I have to laugh.

"Is this is any of your business?" I blast down Hatherly Road.

"He's my brother in law. *And I wanted to fuck you.*" I reach to feel the ribbons of her hair, but she yanks away.

I turn onto Main Street. We arrive at the liquor store, the lights still on. The door unlocked, the cashier gives us a disappointed but understanding look, "I'm about to close."

"A cold bottle of Veuve Clicquot please," Giselle asks. "And some matches."

The cashier hands her a bottle of $120 champagne as I pass him a twenty-five-dollar bottle of Jack Daniels and he rings it up. She extends two hundred-dollar bills, but I push her hand aside and pay.

Back in the car, she rages on. "Secondly you're a married man. Unless you forgot about that."

"He's married."

"Really? I didn't know that."

"Of course you did. Who do you think that big Whale is with him all the time?"

Giselle turns away, "The nanny?"

"No. His wife."

I wish she'd masterfully uncork the champagne bottle with her teeth and spit the cork out while miraculously catching all of the froth in her mouth. But she doesn't do that. She sits there placidly, glancing out the window at the dark marshes. I turn down a side road, to Rocky Hill Beach.

"What are you doing?" she's alarmed.

"I want to show you another beach."

"No. Take me back." I park the car in the beach parking area.

"But we could sit by a fire on the beach. I could assume my Captain Morgan stance above you, just in case you feel compelled to give someone a blow job. We could go skinny dipping."

"I don't like skinny dipping."

"Liar. I saw you skinny dipping on Miner's Beach."

"Doesn't mean I liked it."

"Don't you want to get naked?"

She laughs, "I've been naked enough today."

"Okay but you're really missing out," I advise.

I find myself singing, "I . . . I love the colorful clothes she wears . . . . and the way the sunlight plays upon her hair . . . . She's giving me good vibrations . . ."

But Giselle doesn't sing along.

"Take me home!" She orders.

"I'm the one who just bought you a bottle of the most expensive champagne on earth," I remind her.

"Your family and flock are staying in my rental townhouse, and you'd better not press your luck."

Just then, a blue flashing light pulses behind me, and a police officer taps on my window.

71 Lessons Learned

Not a drop of wine left in the house. Only a large bottle of Amaretto. Candy unwinds the waxy seal on the square bottle and pours into paper cups.

"Didja ever hear of a book called "Sex Tips for Straight Women by a Gay Man"?

"Why the fuck would I know about a crazy book like that?"

"Candy you gotta fucking read that book. Teaches you how to give a great blow job and a great hand job."

"Hand job? Oh fuck me."

"Oh stop acting so innocent, for Christ's sake. You don't fucking give Richard hand jobs? It's time you learnt!"

"You're right. Time I fucking learnt." Candy appears defeated. A thought occurs to me.

I race over to her refrigerator and remove a tube of Pillsbury Sugar Cookie dough. "See? Pretend this is a man's cock."

"Big."

"That's right. A nice big hard one." I hold it up. "Now, you start to squeeze it like this," I demonstrate. She's looking at me like I'm a pervert. "Honest! This is all in the book. The author encourages women to practice on cookie dough."

"You can't be fuckin' serious."

"I'm not fuckin' kidding you Candy, and you better get serious about sex, because you guys are really missing out. Shit!"

"Okay, I guess you're right."

"Hey, if he ain't getting it from you, he's getting it somewhere else, right?"

That's the last clear conversation I can remember of the evening, I recall demonstrating how to perform a hand job on the cookie dough. I recall Candy determinedly working the cookie dough. We did this time and time again, shadows of both of us gleefully toasting paper cups of the liquer, whole-heartedly and gustily, we robustly toasted to ourselves and our children and to better blow jobs and then everything goes black.

I wake up to the piercing blades of seagull calls, in that mealy old bed in Beach Rock Cottage, Candy snores next to me. My head resounds with pain. Even to move one fraction, brings torrents of knives through my temples. My mouth a dry cavern of cotton and bile, I attempt to sit up, but that brings a tidal wave of stones and sand sifting through my brain from my forehead, so remain still. I realize I'm clutching a roll of cookie dough.

Excedrin. Alka Seltzer . . . . Coke . . .

A hand touches mine. It's my little Jack. "Mum! Are you all right?"

"I will be honey, I just need to lay here."

"Yeah but for how long?" His eyes take me in. Given his facial expression, I must look hideous.

"Until I feel better."

"Well, when will that be?"

"I need some Excedrin and some Alka Seltzer and my sunglasses. And my toothbrush . . . And a can of Coke . . ."

"Okay. I'll tell Uncle Richard to go get you some."

"Tell your Dad."

"We can't find him."

"You can't find your Dad?"

"Nope. But Mum, you got to hurry up because that Old Crazy Lady is mad at you."

"Why?"

"She wants you to get out of her house."

"All of our stuff is out of there."

'No it's not, Mom. We left stuff upstairs and the kayak."

"What time is it?"

"That's why she's mad. It's noon."

72 L.A. Woman

The Wintusket Town Jail is small but sturdy, built in 1958 with a flat roof and the pale yellow interior tile of the day. The holding cell is tiny, with one toilet, explicitly made for men, and not me. Luckily, the station camera jammed so they were unable to take mug shots of me. The station was sophisticated enough to accept the American Express Card, which covered my release. They didn't have me on much. I wasn't operating the vehicle. I carried no illegal substances and my champagne bottle was unopened. They kept the American pussy hound and let me go. The officers drove me to the Curtis House, where I packed my things and left, driving my Range Rover to Logan Airport, never to return to this strange little town ever again. Oh, and I found this lovely bracelet.

73 Homeward Bound

Jack Junior brings me the Excedrin and a cold Coke. My intake of these nourishments is slow and painful, but Jack Junior waits, refilling my water glass and keeping the twins at bay as they expand their soap opera to include Little Pet shop characters.

Madison is caring for Austin.

Candy is still down for the count.

Richard is between houses, sorting through two families' belongings, carrying boxes and bags to our cars.

Jack is missing. But he's never there.

And the clock ticks down to one in the afternoon, I've made it downstairs and I'm packing the last of the items in Red Rock Cottage. That's when Betty Ross arrives. I put on my sunglasses before she can get a good look at my eyes.

"I see you're still alive."

"Just barely." I whisper. "What should I do with all this left-over food?"

"Leave it. The house cleaners live on that stuff." She shifts uncomfortably. "Your husband is in the town jail. DUI."

I won't let myself fall apart here, in front of the woman. I'll be home soon, where I can pop a few Lexapro and lose it in the privacy of my own bedroom.

"Really? Well. Can't say I'm surprised." I close the refrigerator. "He's a big boy. He's a lawyer. So he'll figure it out."

Betty's mouth is a thin line of distaste. "He's a tough one to be married to, I imagine."

"Hey. It's tough to be married, period." I laugh, hollowly.

"Hope you enjoyed your week on the beach," Betty smiles wanly.

Saying nothing, I throw my Tori Burch bag over one shoulder and slip my aching feet into my Ugg boots.

"Have a safe trip home!" She waves from the door.

The moment I descend the porch stairs, a bevy of Brazilian housekeepers lug themselves up the stairs, carrying shop vacs and Windex and paper towels. The smell of their cigarettes makes me retch. I take a sip of my Coke and shudder.

In the driveway, Richard slides the last of the twin's hula hoops on top of the pile in the back and closes the back hatch. "Ready to go Marce. Gas tank is full." Hands on his hips, he seems more confident somehow. There's something different about my brother; I can't quite put my finger on.

"Thanks for loading that up for me, Bro." I reach to hug him, he kisses the top of my head. "No problem, little sis. Drive carefully."

"You too," I walk around, put my purse and things on the passenger front seat, and close the door. "When are you leaving?"

Richard shrugs, "Candy's showering over at Curtis House, then we'll be on our way."

"I don't think she's ever drunken that much in her whole life. Really. We never even drank that much in college."

"I can't leave you two alone ever again." Richard laughs.

I climb in behind the wheel and start the engine, "Everybody buckled in?"

"Yes Mom!"

Richard reaches through the window, tiredly, "Do we have to do this again next summer?" His eyes lock with mine as he loosely holds my hand.

"We'll talk about it at Thanksgiving," I smile, squeeze his hand, after a final peck on the cheek, Richard's waving good-bye in the rear view mirror.

"Is it true that Daddy's in jail Mom? Jack Junior asks.

"No, of course not!" I laugh.

74 Dick Control

With a few phone calls, I managed to snake my way out of the DUI conviction. But still.

My dick reminds me he didn't have the pleasure of Giselle's pussy.

On the drive back to New Jersey, my dick reminds me that I've successfully driven Gwen away, based on her final voice mail and the fact that her cell phone numbe is no more.

I think of Jack Junior. "Are you together with Mom, or . . ."

I remind my dick of Marcie's tight, shaved pussy, and then . . . .

I tell my dick who's boss.

75 The Fat Lady Sings

Unpacked. Kids are asleep. Air conditioner humming on the highest level of cool, Richard sets his alarm and pulls back the covers.

"Sure is good to be back in our own bed," I smile. I surrepticiously watch him, removing my reading glasses and closing *Redbook* magazine. I leave my light on so I can see what I'm doing.

"Back to the grind," he sighs and turns off his bedside lamp. I slide closer to him, until I'm against his back. His back flinches.

"What?" he wonders. "What . . . are you . . . ?"

"I'm not tired," I whisper. I'm trying to sound alluring. Sexy.

"Candy, I uh . . . I mean you uh, you should be tired." Richard's breath quickens.

Whispering, "I'm not . . . sleepy." Pulling up my nightgown, I rub my front against his back. Richard tenses up.

"What are you . . . doing?" Richard's caught off guard, and I sigh, pulling down the front of his pajama pants from behind. "CANDY! What are you . . . ?"

He rolls over to face me, a little panicky. "What's this . . . ?"

"I just wanted . . . to see if you . . . wanted me?"

I pull down the covers and slide to where his penis is on eye-level. Just like the book instructions, kneeling over his crotch, I put my hands on his penis, lifting it, like Marcie directed, and I put it in my mouth.

"Oh my God, Candy." he sighs, but Richard's not relaxed yet, I can tell. His penis is still soft.

I lift my head and come back down hard.

"No teeth!" he whispers. He's not hardening.

"Candy. What are you doing? . . ."

"Just relax!" As I take him into my left hand, and then with my right, I gather up his balls in my palm and gently knead them, squeezing them . . . I almost giggle when I recall practicing this on a roll of cookie dough. It's a little like pizza dough, when you're making calzones, I think.

He's still not getting hard, so I knead his balls a little harder. "Take it easy!" he flinches.

What am I doing wrong?

I look down in the bedside light, sliding his cock with my left hand and kneading his balls with my right, I notice his privates are shimmery, so I get a closer look. His balls are covered with silver glitter, everywhere. Silver glitter in the creases of his balls, sprinkled in his pubic hair, adorning the tip of his cock. Up the sides.

"Richard, there's silver glitter all over you . . . Where'd you get glitter . . . ?"

Dazed, distracted, Richard raises his neck, "Glitter?"

I let go of Richard's parts and skuttle to the foot of the bed, pulling down my nightgown.

"Richard. Where'd all that glitter come from?"

Richard sits up, struggling to put on his glasses. "The twins were doing an . . . an art project? Arts and crafts. Spilled all over my lap . . ."

"There's glitter all over your privates."

". . . And some kid's soap they left in the shower . . . from the beach house, I didn't realize . . . must of picked it up in the shower!"

"Glitter on your privates." *As I say the words, the full voltage of the reality hits me and I take a long breath. I pull my nightgown over myself.*

And then I flash on the Australian woman's fingernails.

"You cheat!"

"What?"

"You cheated on me with that Australian whore!"

He doesn't hug me or try to comfort me, he just gets out of bed, weighing the circumstances, his eyes avoid me. "I don't know what you're talking about."

"That Australian woman with the fake silver glitter nails! The proof is all over you." He unbuttons his pajama top and pulls on a polo shirt.

"Why all of a sudden, are you interested in sex?" he asks, his face, stone.

"Well, Marcie and I were talking about it, and I thought it might make you happy."

"Candy, you *just out of the blue,* decide to suddenly have sex, after how many years? To go down on me? You've never—"

"Well, apparently some one else did it for me!—"

"Don't."

"Look at your cock? It's covered with glitter! You had sex with that woman!"

"Hey! At least somebody in this marriage is finally having sex."

"I would have done it . . . if you'd ask."

"When was I supposed to ask?"

"Whenever."

"I shouldn't have to ask! It should be natural."

"All of this is because of the diabetic thing I suppose . . ."

"Well, it certainly contributes to the subject!"

"What is the subject?"

"The subject is . . . what are we doing here? Candy, I mean, what are we doing here?"

"Shhh! Don't wake up the kids."

"No I mean it Candy. What are we doing here? Playing house? Room mates? Bunk mates? This marriage sucks!"

"How can you say that? When all I do I wait on you, hand and foot—"

"Oh, we serve each other! We carve pumpkins! We belong to the Canoe Club! The Christmas decorations and the school fundraisers and we have dinner on Valentine's Day but we never, ever FUCK!"

"Well, I guess I was busy with the karate and tennis lessons, CCD and the orthodontist and getting the oil changed and stripping the beds and making the kids study for finals and washing the curtains and the blood drive and whooping cough vaccinations and tetanus shots and—"

"So the kids won't get malaria! So what! You gave them diabetes!"

"How dare you!"

"You work hard at everything that doesn't matter!"

"So sue me!"

"You have gotten everything you wanted! I'm sick of giving!"

"Oh so you're saying you want a divorce?"

Richard has put on his jeans, loafers, thrown on a jacket, and grabs his car keys. He turns, yet he can't look at me. He throws a few things into his gym bag.

I'm crying, begging, "Richard. Don't you want to try . . . ?"

"No Candy. I don't." And with that, Richard leaves me.

76 Homecoming

The twins and Jack Junior are snuggled half asleep on the couch with popcorn and a movie when I hear the roar of Jack's Porsche in the driveway.

I straighten myself up and look in the mirror. I fix my runny mascara and tame my frizz with a brush. I hear him hit the marble foyer with his long strides. My heart drops like a stone when I hear him taking the marble winding steps two at a time, "My Marcie! Where's my Marcie?"

Jack bursts through the bathroom door, tosses his bag on the floor, and hugs me and dips me so far down that I fight off vertigo. I talk slowly. My voice is dead. "Where you been?"

"Busy, very busy," he laughs. It's a false laugh. I guess I never listened hard enough to hear how fake it is.

I brush his bangs aside and stare into those mesmerizing pale green eyes.

"Must have used your Get Out of Jail Free card, eh?"

Jack's eyes waver, slightly. And maybe because I'm so hungover my teeth hurt, but now, today, I can see the lies.

I feel his right wrist. The bracelet is gone. My heart sinks further. "So where's the bracelet I gave you?" I ask.

"The bracelet!" he flashes me that million dollar smile, feels both his wrists, feels his pockets, "Hang on. It's some where."

"You lost my bracelet. Jack. Did you leave it at the jail? Or in Gwen's apartment?" Beyond angry, I can feel him leaving me, with every breath.

"No! It's in the car." Jack flies down the stairs. I watch out the bedroom window as approaches his real baby, his beloved Porsche. The top is down. He opens the driver's side door, sits in the driver's seat. I spy him opening the glove compartment, digging around, then slowly closing the glove box door. He's remembering something. I know Jack's movements. Jack knows where his bracelet is. And apparently, it's not where it's supposed to be.

I watch Jack scratch his head, cup his chin, as he slowly gets out of the car and paces. He raises his phone, thinks better of it, and replaces it in his pocket. While his brain begins to formulate counter arguments and alibis, I open his closet door. I remove his chocolate suede Georgio Armani sport jacket, a prize possession, worth God knows what. Remove it from the hanger. From above, I drop the jacket off the bedroom balcony. It lands on the trunk of Jack's Porsche with a thump.

"What the hell?" He spins and looks up at me, mouth open, knitted brow. "What're you doing?"

"I'm packing for you."

"What?" I retrieve Jack's vacation bag. "Marcie? What the eff?"

"Here's your bag!" Wham. His bag hits the hood.

"Marcie! What're you doing?" His Asshole Voice.

I lean on the balcony. "Jack—go check into a hotel. I need time to think." I close and lock the French doors and pick up the phone to call my lawyer.

77 Beach Amateurs

She has a beach umbrella. On a windy day! *How stupid can she be? Where do these people come from? Who teaches them?*

The idiot weakly drives the stake end into the sand, not near deep enough, unfurls the umbrella, and then sits on her fat kiester in a beach chair, thinking she's going to read *The Boston Globe* in this wind.

There are white cap waves, a small craft warning, and this imbecilic woman raises a beach umbrella! It has a sharp metal shaft.

"Take that down!" I warn her from afar.

She does nothing, but I'll get her.

"Take that umbrella down before it stabs someone!" I'm getting closer. Her newspaper fights the breeze, while she struggles, I get closer.

"Take that down!"

She finally comprehends that I'm talking to her. "Me?" she questions and points to herself.

"That umbrella! Take it down!" I'm gasping, it's taken so much energy to get over there, and still she sits on her fanny.

"Can I help you?" Her neck goes back in affrontery.

Just then, the wind lifts the umbrella, flips it over twice and the sharp point impales a watermelon on a nearby picnic table.

"See! I told you!" I'm huffing and puffing. Pain, pain everywhere. In my arms, my back, my neck. *But this is my beach. My beach!*

The woman apologetically stumbles to fetch the umbrella, as her beach chair and newspaper go flying, and then she re-sets the umbrella in the same fashion as before. I go over, grab the umbrella, I close it and set it down flat and stand on it. I'm coughing out my words.

The woman, fat and stupid glares at me, "Excuse me? Who do you think you are! I brought this to protect my children from the sun!"

"Well they're certainly not under it." I look around for her children, but people and colors are a blur.

"Listen lady—I don't need your permission to put this up!" she stands righteously, fat and stupid.

I laugh. And cough out the words, *"This is my land. My beach!"*

"Whoever you are, go away!" The feeling of a seawall, as heavy as cement, on my chest. Pressing me down, to the ground . . . the idiot threatens, "I'll call the police!"

I rasp, hacking, "Call the police! They'll tell you this is my land, my beach!—"

78 Wishful Thinking

"In a spectacular collapse while preventing a family from putting up a beach umbrella on a windy day, Gloria Briggs suffered a massive stroke on the beloved beach where she was born in 1920 . . ."

"You can't say that in an obituary, Tiffany," Betty Ross instructs. "Not to mention my dear, she's not even dead yet."

"I know. Wishful thinking!" Tiffany laughs, tossing her first draft into the trash. "The whole town is celebrating."

"Prematurely, I may add. Should at least wait until they pull the plug on her. Oh and Tiff. Have you gotten a hold of her son yet?"

"He signed all the papers. They're gone to Mexico."

"Splendid." With a precise eye for real estate photography, Betty studies the photographs, the angles of the three houses, the lighting of the beach, the overhead shot of the peninsula of Brigg's Beach. "These look great."

"So I can email the JPEGs to The New York Times?" Tiffany looks up from her laptop.

"Go ahead." Betty tapes the photos to the lobby window, facing out to passersby. Immediately, a couple stops and points at the captivating aerial photograph.

Tiffany presses 'send.' "This is exciting, Mrs. Ross."

Betty nods and looks above to thank the heavens, "It'll be the most desirable compound on the East Coast! And the Kennedys think they have a compound! Ha."

Tiffany's bare shoulders surge with excitement at the prospect. "It'll attract some heavy hitter. Maybe a Hollywood director. Or Oprah. Wouldn't that be something?"

"Indeed, it would, but at the moment, I need you to make me a bloody mary. And one for yourself, of course."

"Thank you, Mrs. Ross. We deserve it."

Betty smiles mysteriously, shaking her head, dropping into her chair. "Yes we do. *Whew! What a week.*"

THE END

About Cab Doyle

Former advertising creative director and screenwriter,
"A Week on the Beach" is Mr. Doyle's first novel.